THE LITTLE LAME PRINCE
AND
THE ADVENTURES OF A BROWNIE

DINAH MARIA MULOCK

THE LITTLE LAME PRINCE

AND

THE ADVENTURES OF A BROWNIE

ILLUSTRATED BY

COLLEEN BROWNING

CHILDREN'S CLASSICS

GARDEN CITY, NEW YORK

Inscribed

WITH DEEP TENDERNESS

TO A DEAR LITTLE BOY I KNOW

1874   D.M.M.

CONTENTS

THE LITTLE LAME PRINCE

CHAPTER ONE

Yes, he was the most beautiful Prince that ever was born.

Of course, being a Prince, people said this: but it was true besides. When he looked at the candle, his eyes had an expression of earnest inquiry quite startling in a new-born baby. His nose—there was not much of it certainly, but what there was seemed an aquiline shape; his complexion was a charming, healthy purple; he was round and fat, straight-limbed and long—in fact, a splendid baby, and everybody was exceedingly proud of him. Especially his father and mother, the King and Queen of Nomansland, who had waited for him during their happy reign of ten years—now made happier than ever, to themselves and their subjects, by the appearance of a son and heir.

The only person who was not quite happy was the King's brother, the heir-presumptive, who would have been king one day, had the baby not been born. But as his Majesty was very kind to him, and even rather sorry for him—insomuch that at the Queen's request he gave him a dukedom almost as big as a county—the Crown Prince, as he was called, tried to seem pleased also; and let us hope he succeeded.

The Prince's christening was to be a grand affair. According to the custom of the country, there were chosen for him four-and-twenty godfathers and godmothers, who each had to give him a name, and promise to do their utmost for him. When he came of age, he himself had to choose the name—and the godfather or godmother—that he liked best, for the rest of his days.

Meantime, all was rejoicing. Subscriptions were made among the rich to give pleasure to the poor: dinners in town-halls for the working men; tea-parties in the streets for their wives; and milk and bun feasts for the children in the schoolrooms. For Nomansland, though I cannot point it out in any map, or read of it in any history, was, I believe, much like our own or many another country.

As for the palace—which was no different from other palaces—it was clean "turned out of the windows," as people say, with the preparations going on. The only quiet place in it was the room which, though the Prince was six weeks old, his mother the Queen had never quitted. Nobody said she was ill, however; it would have been so inconvenient; and as she said nothing about it herself, but lay pale and placid, giving no trouble to anybody, nobody thought much about her. All the world was absorbed in admiring the baby.

The christening-day came at last, and it was as lovely as the Prince himself. All the people in the palace were lovely too— or thought themselves so, in the elegant new clothes which the Queen, who thought of everybody, had taken care to give them, from the ladies-in-waiting down to the poor little kitchenmaid, who looked at herself in her pink cotton gown, and thought, doubtless, that there never was such a pretty girl as she.

By six in the morning all the royal household had dressed itself in its very best; and then the little Prince was dressed in his best—his magnificent christening-robe; which proceeding his Royal Highness did not like at all, but kicked and screamed like any common baby. When he had a little calmed down, they carried him to be looked at by the Queen his mother, who, though her royal robes had been brought and laid upon the bed, was, as everybody well knew, quite unable to rise and put them on.

She admired her baby very much; kissed and blessed him, and lay looking at him, as she did for hours sometimes, when he was placed beside her fast asleep; then she gave him up with a gentle smile, and saying, "she hoped he would be very good, that it would be a very nice christening, and all the guests would enjoy themselves," turned peacefully over on her bed, saying nothing more to anybody. She was a very uncomplaining person—the Queen, and her name was Dolorez.

Everything went on exactly as if she had been present. All, even the King himself, had grown used to her absence, for she was not strong, and for years had not joined in any gaieties. She always did her royal duties, but as to pleasures, they could go on quite well without her, or it seemed so. The company arrived: great and notable persons in this and neighbouring countries; also the four-and-twenty godfathers and godmothers, who had been chosen with care, as the people who would be most useful to his Royal Highness, should he ever want friends, which did not seem likely. What such want could possibly happen to the heir of the powerful monarch of Nomansland?

They came, walking two and two, with their coronets on their heads—being dukes and duchesses, princes and princesses, or the like; they all kissed the child, and pronounced the name which each had given him. Then the four-and-twenty names were shouted out with great energy by six heralds, one after the other, and afterwards written down, to be preserved in the state records, in readiness for the next time they were wanted, which would be either on his Royal Highness's coronation or his funeral. Soon the ceremony was over, and everybody satisfied; except, perhaps, the little Prince himself, who moaned faintly under his christening robes, which nearly smothered him.

In truth, though very few knew, the Prince in coming to the chapel had met with a slight disaster. His nurse—not his ordinary one, but the state nursemaid, an elegant and fashionable young lady of rank, whose duty it was to carry him to and from the chapel, had been so occupied in arranging her train with one hand, while she held the baby with the other, that she stumbled and let him fall, just at the foot of the marble staircase. To be sure, she contrived to pick him up again the next minute; and the accident was so slight it seemed hardly worth speaking of. Consequently, nobody did speak of it. The baby had turned deadly pale but did not cry, so no person a step or two behind could discover anything wrong; afterwards, even if he had moaned, the silver trumpets were loud enough to drown his voice. It would have been a pity to let anything trouble such a day of felicity.

So, after a minute's pause, the procession had moved on. Such a procession! Heralds in blue and silver; pages in crimson and gold; and a troop of little girls in dazzling white, carrying baskets of flowers, which they strewed all the way before the nurse and child—finally the four-and-twenty godfathers and godmothers, as proud as possible, and so splendid to look at that they would have quite extinguished their small godson— merely a heap of lace and muslin with a baby-face inside—had it not been for a canopy of white satin and ostrich feathers, which was held over him wherever he was carried.

Thus, with the sun shining on them through the painted windows, they stood; the King and his train on one side, the

Prince and his attendants on the other, as pretty a sight as ever was seen out of fairyland.

"It's just like fairyland," whispered the eldest little girl to the next eldest, as she shook the last rose out of her basket; "and I think the only thing the Prince wants now is a fairy godmother."

"Does he?" said a shrill but soft and not unpleasant voice behind; and there was seen among the group of children some-body—not a child—yet no bigger than a child: somebody whom nobody had seen before, and who certainly had not been in-vited, for she had no christening clothes on.

She was a little old woman dressed all in grey: grey gown; grey hooded cloak, of a material excessively fine, and a tint that seemed perpetually changing, like the grey of an evening sky. Her hair was grey, and her eyes also; even her complexion had a soft grey shadow over it. But there was nothing unpleasantly old about her, and her smile was as sweet and childlike as the Prince's own, which stole over his pale little face the instant she came near enough to touch him.

"Take care. Don't let the baby fall again."

The grand young lady nurse started, flushing angrily.

"Who spoke to me? How did anybody know? I mean, what business has anybody——?" Then, frightened, but still speak-ing in a much sharper tone than I hope young ladies of rank are in the habit of speaking—"Old woman, you will be kind enough not to say 'the baby,' but 'the Prince.' Keep away; his Royal Highness is just going to sleep."

"Nevertheless, I must kiss him. I am his godmother."

"You!" cried the elegant lady nurse.

"You!!" repeated all the gentlemen and ladies-in-waiting.

"You!!!" echoed the heralds and pages—and they began

to blow the silver trumpets, in order to stop all further conversation.

The Prince's procession formed itself for returning—the King and his train having already moved off towards the palace—but, on the topmost step of the marble stairs, stood, right in front of all, the little old woman clothed in grey.

She stretched herself on tiptoe by the help of her stick, and gave the little Prince three kisses.

"This is intolerable," cried the young lady nurse, wiping the kisses off rapidly with her lace handkerchief. "Such an insult to his Royal Highness. Take yourself out of the way, old woman, or the King shall be informed immediately."

"The King knows nothing of me, more's the pity," replied the old woman with an indifferent air, as if she thought the loss was more on his Majesty's side than hers. "My friend in the palace is the King's wife."

"Kings' wives are called queens," said the lady nurse, with a contemptuous air.

"You are right," replied the old woman. "Nevertheless, I know her Majesty well, and I love her and her child. And—since you dropped him on the marble stairs (this she said in a mysterious whisper, which made the young lady tremble in spite of her anger)—I choose to take him for my own. I am his godmother, ready to help him whenever he wants me."

"You help him!" cried all the group, breaking into shouts of laughter, to which the little old woman paid not the slightest attention. Her soft grey eyes were fixed on the Prince, who seemed to answer to the look, smiling again and again in causeless, aimless fashion, as babies do smile.

"His Majesty must hear of this," said a gentleman-in-waiting.

"His Majesty will hear quite enough news in a minute or two," said the old woman sadly. And again stretching up to the little Prince, she kissed him on the forehead solemnly.

"Be called by a new name which nobody has ever thought of. Be Prince Dolor, in memory of your mother Dolorez."

"In memory of!" Everybody started at the ominous phrase, and also at a most terrible breach of etiquette which the old woman had committed. In Nomansland, neither the king nor the queen were supposed to have any Christian name at all. They dropped it on their coronation-day, and it was never mentioned again till it was engraved on their coffins when they died.

"Old woman, you are exceedingly ill-bred," cried the eldest lady-in-waiting, much horrified. "How you could know the fact passes my comprehension. But even if you did not know it, how dared you presume to hint that her most gracious Majesty is called Dolorez?"

"*Was* called Dolorez," said the old woman with a tender solemnity.

The first gentleman, called the Gold-stick-in-waiting, raised it to strike her, and all the rest stretched out their hands to seize her; but the grey mantle melted from between their fingers like air; and, before anybody had time to do anything more, there came a heavy, muffled, startling sound.

The great bell of the palace—the bell which was only heard on the death of some of the Royal family, and for as many times as he or she was years old—began to toll. They listened, mute and horror-stricken. Some one counted: one—two—three—four—up to nine and twenty—just the Queen's age.

It was, indeed, the Queen. Her Majesty was dead! In the midst of the festivities she had slipped away, out of her new happiness and her old sufferings, neither few nor small. Sending away her women to see the sight—at least, they said afterwards, in excuse, that she had done so, and it was very like her to do it—she had turned with her face to the window, whence one could just see the tops of the distant mountains—the Beautiful Mountains, as they were called—where she was born. So gazing, she had quietly died.

When the little Prince was carried back to his mother's room, there was no mother to kiss him. And, though he did not know it, there would be for him no mother's kiss any more.

As for his godmother—the little old woman in grey who called herself so—whether she melted into air, like her gown when they touched it, or whether she flew out of the chapel window, or slipped through the doorway among the bewildered crowd, nobody knew—nobody ever thought about her.

Only the nurse, the ordinary homely one, coming out of the Prince's nursery in the middle of the night in search of a cordial to quiet his continual moans, saw, sitting in the doorway, something which she would have thought a mere shadow, had she not seen shining out of it two eyes, grey and soft and sweet. She put her hand before her own, screaming loudly. When she took them away, the old woman was gone.

CHAPTER TWO

Everybody was very kind to the poor little Prince. I think people generally are kind to motherless children, whether princes or peasants. He had a magnificent nursery, and a regular suite of attendants, and was treated with the greatest respect and state. Nobody was allowed to talk to him in silly baby language, or dandle him, or, above all, to kiss him, though, perhaps, some people did it surreptitiously, for he was such a sweet baby that it was difficult to help it.

It could not be said that the Prince missed his mother; children of his age cannot do that; but somehow after she died everything seemed to go wrong with him. From a beautiful baby he became sickly and pale, seeming to have almost ceased growing, especially in his legs, which had been so fat and strong. But after the day of his christening they withered and shrank; he no longer kicked them out either in passion or play, and when, as he got to be nearly a year old, his nurse tried to make him stand upon them, he only tumbled down.

This happened so many times, that at last people began to talk about it. A Prince, and not able to stand on his own legs! What a dreadful thing! what a misfortune for the country!

Rather a misfortune to him also, poor little boy! but nobody seemed to think of that. And when, after a while, his health revived, and the old bright look came back to his sweet little face, and his body grew larger and stronger, though still his legs remained the same, people continued to speak of him in whispers, and with grave shakes of the head. Everybody knew, though nobody said it, that something, impossible to guess what, was not quite right with the poor little Prince.

Of course, nobody hinted this to the King his father: it does not do to tell great people anything unpleasant. And besides, his Majesty took very little notice of his son, or of his other affairs, beyond the necessary duties of his kingdom. People had said he would not miss the Queen at all, she having been so long an invalid: but he did. After her death he never was quite the same. He established himself in her empty rooms, the only rooms in the palace whence one could see the Beautiful Mountains, and was often observed looking at them as if he thought she had flown away thither, and that his longing could bring her back again. And by a curious coincidence, which nobody dared to inquire into, he desired that the Prince might be called, not by any of the four-and-twenty grand names given him by his godfathers and godmothers, but by the identical name mentioned by the little old woman in grey—Dolor, after his mother Dolorez.

Once a week, according to established state custom, the Prince, dressed in his very best, was brought to the King, his father, for half-an-hour, but his Majesty was generally too ill and too melancholy to pay much heed to the child.

Only once, when he and the Crown Prince, who was exceedingly attentive to his royal brother, were sitting together, with Prince Dolor playing in a corner of the room, dragging himself about with his arms rather than his legs, and sometimes trying feebly to crawl from one chair to another, it seemed to strike the father that all was not right with his son.

"How old is his Royal Highness?" said he suddenly to the nurse.

"Two years, three months, and five days, please your Majesty."

"It does not please me," said the King with a sigh. "He ought to be far more forward than he is now, ought he not, brother? You, who have so many children, must know. Is there not something wrong about him?"

"Oh, no," said the Crown Prince, exchanging meaning looks with the nurse, who did not understand at all, but stood frightened and trembling with the tears in her eyes. "Nothing to make your Majesty at all uneasy. No doubt his Royal Highness will outgrow it in time."

"Outgrow—what?"

"A slight delicacy—ahem!—in the spine; something inherited, perhaps, from his dear mother."

"Ah, she was always delicate; but she was the sweetest woman that ever lived. Come here, my little son."

And as the Prince turned round upon his father a small, sweet, grave face—so like his mother's—his Majesty the King smiled and held out his arms. But when the boy came to him, not running like a boy, but wriggling awkwardly along the floor, the royal countenance clouded over.

"I ought to have been told of this. It is terrible—terrible! And for a Prince too! Send for all the doctors in my kingdom immediately."

They came, and each gave a different opinion, and ordered a different mode of treatment. The only thing they agreed in was what had been pretty well known before: that the Prince must have been hurt when he was an infant—let fall, perhaps, so as to injure his spine and lower limbs. Did nobody remember?

No, nobody. Indignantly, all the nurses denied that any such accident had happened, was possible to have happened, until the faithful country nurse recollected that it really had happened, on the day of the christening. For which unlucky good memory, all the others scolded her so severely that she had no peace of her life, and soon after, by the influence of the young lady nurse who had carried the baby that fatal day, and who was a sort of connection of the Crown Prince, being his wife's second cousin once removed, the poor woman was pensioned off, and sent to the Beautiful Mountains, from whence she came, with orders to remain there for the rest of her days.

But of all this the King knew nothing, for, indeed, after the first shock of finding out that his son could not walk, and seemed never likely to walk, he interfered very little concerning him. The whole thing was too painful, and his Majesty had never liked painful things. Sometimes he inquired after Prince Dolor, and they told him his Royal Highness was going on as well as could be expected, which really was the case. For after worrying the poor child and perplexing themselves with one remedy after another, the Crown Prince, not wishing to offend any of the differing doctors, had proposed leaving him to nature; and nature, the safest doctor of all, had come to his help, and done her best. He could not walk, it is true; his limbs were mere useless additions to his body; but the body itself was strong and sound. And his face was the same as ever—just his mother's face, one of the sweetest in the world!

Even the King, indifferent as he was, sometimes looked at the little fellow with sad tenderness, noticing how cleverly he learned to crawl, and swing himself about by his arms, so that in his own awkward way he was as active in motion as most children of his age.

"Poor little man! He does his best, and he is not unhappy;

not half so unhappy as I, brother," addressing the Crown Prince, who was more constant than ever in his attendance upon the sick monarch. "If anything should befall me, I have appointed you as Regent. In case of my death, you will take care of my poor little boy?"

"Certainly, certainly; but do not let us imagine any such misfortune. I assure your Majesty—everybody will assure you—that it is not in the least likely."

He knew, however, and everybody knew, that it was likely, and soon after it actually did happen. The King died, as suddenly and quietly as the Queen had done—indeed, in her very room and bed; and Prince Dolor was left without either father or mother—as sad a thing as could happen, even to a Prince.

He was more than that now, though. He was a King. In Nomansland, as in other countries, the people were struck with grief one day and revived the next. "The King is dead—long live the King!" was the cry that rang through the nation, and almost before his late Majesty had been laid beside the Queen in their splendid mausoleum, crowds came thronging from all parts to the royal palace, eager to see the new monarch.

They did see him—the Prince Regent took care they should —sitting on the floor of the council-chamber, sucking his thumb! And when one of the gentlemen-in-waiting lifted him up and carried him—fancy, carrying a King!—to the chair of state, and put the crown on his head, he shook it off again, it was so heavy and uncomfortable. Sliding down to the foot of the throne, he began playing with the golden lions that supported it, stroking their paws and putting his tiny fingers into their eyes, and laughing—laughing as if he had at last found something to amuse him.

"There's a fine king for you!" said the first lord-in-waiting, a friend of the Prince Regent's (the Crown Prince that used to be, who, in the deepest mourning, stood silently beside the throne of his young nephew. He was a handsome man, very grand and clever looking). "What a king, who can never stand to receive his subjects, never walk in processions, who, to the last day of his life, will have to be carried about like a baby! Very unfortunate!"

"Exceedingly unfortunate," repeated the second lord. "It is always bad for a nation when its king is a child; but such a child—a permanent cripple, if not worse."

"Let us hope not worse," said the first lord in a very hopeless tone, and looking towards the Regent, who stood erect and pretended to hear nothing. "I have heard that these sort of children with very large heads and great broad foreheads and staring eyes, are—well, well, let us hope for the best and be prepared for the worst. In the meantime——"

"I swear," said the Crown Prince, coming forward and kissing the hilt of his sword—"I swear to perform my duties as Regent, to take all care of his Royal Highness—his Majesty, I mean," with a grand bow to the little child, who laughed innocently back again. "And I will do my humble best to govern the country. Still, if the country has the slightest objection——"

But the Crown Prince being generalissimo, and having the whole army at his beck and call, so that he could have begun a civil war in no time; the country had, of course, not the slightest objection.

So the king and queen slept together in peace, and Prince Dolor reigned over the land—that is, his uncle did; and everybody said what a fortunate thing it was for the poor little Prince to have such a clever uncle to take care of him. All things went on as usual; indeed, after the Regent had brought his wife and her seven sons, and established them in the palace, rather better than usual. For they gave such splendid entertainments and made the capital so lively, that trade revived, and the country was said to be more flourishing than it had been for a century.

Whenever the Regent and his sons appeared, they were received with shouts—"Long live the Crown Prince!" "Long live the Royal family!" And, in truth, they were very fine children, the whole seven of them, and made a great show when they rode out together on seven beautiful horses, one height above another, down to the youngest, on his tiny black pony, no bigger than a large dog.

As for the other child, his Royal Highness Prince Dolor—for somehow people soon ceased to call him his Majesty, which seemed such a ridiculous title for a poor little fellow, a helpless cripple, with only head and trunk, and no legs to speak of—he was seen very seldom by anybody.

Sometimes, people daring enough to peer over the high wall of the palace garden, noticed there, carried in a footman's arms, or drawn in a chair, or left to play on the grass, often with nobody to mind him, a pretty little boy, with a bright intelligent face, and large melancholy eyes—no, not exactly melancholy, for they were his mother's, and she was by no means sadminded, but thoughtful and dreamy. They rather perplexed people, those childish eyes; they were so exceedingly innocent and yet so penetrating. If anybody did a wrong thing, told a lie for instance, they would turn round with such a grave silent surprise—the child never talked much—that every naughty person in the palace was rather afraid of Prince Dolor.

He could not help it, and perhaps he did not even know it, being no better a child than many other children, but there was

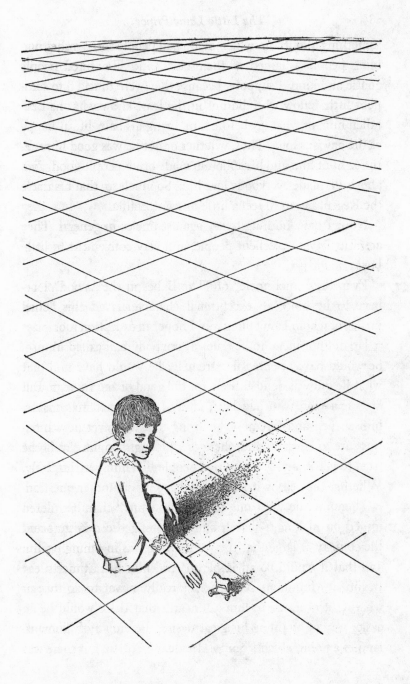

something about him which made bad people sorry, and grumbling people ashamed of themselves, and ill-natured people gentle and kind. I suppose, because they were touched to see a poor little fellow who did not in the least know what had befallen him, or what lay before him, living his baby life as happy as the day was long. Thus, whether or not he was good himself, the sight of him and his affliction made other people good, and, above all, made everybody love him. So much so, that his uncle the Regent began to feel a little uncomfortable.

Now, I have nothing to say against uncles in general. They are usually very excellent people, and very convenient to little boys and girls.

Even the "cruel uncle" of "The Babes in the Wood" I believe to be quite an exceptional character. And this "cruel uncle" of whom I am telling was, I hope, an exception too.

He did not mean to be cruel. If anybody had called him so, he would have resented it extremely: he would have said that what he did was done entirely for the good of the country. But he was a man who had been always accustomed to consider himself first and foremost, believing that whatever he wanted was sure to be right, and, therefore, he ought to have it. So he tried to get it, and got it too, as people like him very often do. Whether they enjoy it when they have it, is another question.

Therefore, he went one day to the council-chamber, determined on making a speech and informing the ministers and the country at large that the young King was in failing health, and that it would be advisable to send him for a time to the Beautiful Mountains. Whether he really meant to do this; or whether it occurred to him afterwards that there would be an easier way of attaining his great desire, the crown of Nomansland, is a point which I cannot decide.

But soon after, when he had obtained an order in council to send the King away—which was done in great state, with a guard of honour composed of two whole regiments of soldiers —the nation learnt, without much surprise, that the poor little Prince—nobody ever called him King now—had gone a much longer journey than to the Beautiful Mountains.

He had fallen ill on the road and died within a few hours; at least, so declared the physician in attendance, and the nurse who had been sent to take care of him. They brought his coffin back in great state, and buried it in the mausoleum with his parents.

So Prince Dolor was seen no more. The country went into deep mourning for him, and then forgot him, and his uncle reigned in his stead. That illustrious personage accepted his crown with great decorum, and wore it with great dignity, to the last. But whether he enjoyed it or not, there is no evidence to show.

CHAPTER THREE

And what of the little lame Prince, whom everybody seemed so easily to have forgotten?

Not everybody. There were a few kind souls, mothers of families, who had heard his sad story, and some servants about the palace, who had been familiar with his sweet ways—these many a time sighed and said "Poor Prince Dolor!" Or, looking at the Beautiful Mountains, which were visible all over Nomansland, though few people ever visited them, "Well, perhaps his Royal Highness is better where he is than even there."

They did not know—indeed, hardly anybody did know—that beyond the mountains, between them and the sea, lay a tract of country, barren, level, bare, except for short stunted grass, and here and there a patch of tiny flowers. Not a bush—not a tree—not a resting-place for bird or beast was in that dreary plain. In summer, the sunshine fell upon it hour after hour with a blinding glare; in winter, the winds and rains swept over it unhindered, and the snow came down, steadily, noiselessly, covering it from end to end in one great white sheet, which lay for days and weeks unmarked by a single footprint.

Not a pleasant place to live in—and nobody did live there, apparently. The only sign that human creatures had ever been near the spot, was one large round tower which rose up in the centre of the plain, and might be seen all over it—if there had been anybody to see, which there never was. Rose, right up out of the ground, as if it had grown of itself, like a mushroom.

But it was not at all mushroom-like; on the contrary, it was very solidly built. In form, it resembled the Irish round towers, which have puzzled people for so long, nobody being able to find out when, or by whom, or for what purpose they were made; seemingly for no use at all, like this tower. It was circular, of very firm brickwork, with neither doors nor windows, until near the top, when you could perceive some slits in the wall, through which one might possibly creep in or look out. Its height was nearly a hundred feet high, and it had a battlemented parapet, showing sharp against the sky.

As the plain was quite desolate—almost like a desert, only without sand, and led to nowhere except the still more desolate sea-coast—nobody ever crossed it. Whatever mystery there was about the tower, it and the sky and the plain kept their secret to themselves.

It was a very great secret indeed—a state secret—which none but so clever a man as the present King of Nomansland would ever have thought of. How he carried it out, undiscovered, I cannot tell. People said, long afterwards, that it was by means of a gang of condemned criminals, who were set to work, and executed immediately after they had done, so that nobody knew anything, or in the least suspected the real fact.

And what was the fact? Why, that this tower, which seemed a mere mass of masonry, utterly forsaken and uninhabited, was not so at all. Within twenty feet of the top, some ingenious architect had planned a perfect little house, divided into four rooms—as by drawing a cross within a circle you will see might easily be done. By making skylights, and a few slits in the walls for windows, and raising a peaked roof which was hidden by the parapet, here was a dwelling complete; eighty feet from the ground, and as inaccessible as a rook's nest on the top of a tree.

A charming place to live in! If you once got up there, and never wanted to come down again.

Inside—though nobody could have looked inside except a bird, and hardly even a bird flew past that lonely tower—inside it was furnished with all the comfort and elegance imaginable; with lots of books and toys, and everything that the heart of a child could desire. For its only inhabitant, except a nurse of course, was a poor little solitary child.

One winter night, when all the plain was white with moonlight, there was seen crossing it a great tall black horse, ridden by a man also big and equally black, carrying before him on the saddle a woman and a child. The woman—she had a sad fierce look, and no wonder, for she was a criminal under sentence of death, but her sentence had been changed to almost as severe a punishment. She was to inhabit the lonely tower with the child, and was allowed to live as long as the child lived—no longer. This, in order that she might take the utmost care of him; for those who put him there were equally afraid of his dying and of his living. And yet he was only a little gentle boy, with a sweet sleepy smile—he had been very tired with his long journey—and clinging arms, which held tight to the man's neck, for he was rather frightened, and the face, black as it was, looked kindly at him. And he was very helpless, with his poor small shrivelled legs, which could neither stand nor run away —for the little forlorn boy was Prince Dolor.

He had not been dead at all—or buried either. His grand funeral had been a mere pretence: a wax figure having been put in his place, while he himself was spirited away under charge of these two, the condemned woman and the black man. The latter was deaf and dumb, so could neither tell nor repeat anything.

When they reached the foot of the tower, there was light enough to see a huge chain dangling from the parapet, but dangling only halfway. The deaf-mute took from his saddle-wallet a sort of ladder, arranged in pieces like a puzzle, fitted it together and lifted it up to meet the chain. Then he mounted to the top of the tower, and slung from it a sort of chair, in which the woman and the child placed themselves and were drawn up, never to come down again as long as they lived. Leaving them there, the man descended the ladder, took it to pieces again and packed it in his pack, mounted the horse, and disappeared across the plain.

Every month they used to watch for him, appearing like a speck in the distance. He fastened his horse to the foot of the tower and climbed it, as before, laden with provisions and many other things. He always saw the Prince, so as to make sure that the child was alive and well, and then went away until the following month.

While his first childhood lasted, Prince Dolor was happy enough. He had every luxury that even a prince could need, and the one thing wanting—love, never having known, he did not miss. His nurse was very kind to him, though she was a wicked woman. But either she had not been quite so wicked as people said, or she grew better through being shut up continually with a little innocent child, who was dependent upon her for every comfort and pleasure of his life.

It was not an unhappy life. There was nobody to tease or ill-use him, and he was never ill. He played about from room to room—there were four rooms, parlour, kitchen, his nurse's bed-room, and his own; learnt to crawl like a fly, and to jump like a frog, and to run about on all-fours almost as fast as a puppy. In fact, he was very much like a puppy or a kitten, as thoughtless and as merry—scarcely ever cross, though sometimes a little weary.

As he grew older, he occasionally liked to be quiet for awhile, and then he would sit at the slits of windows, which were, however, much bigger than they looked from the bottom of the tower—and watch the sky above and the ground below, with the storms sweeping over and the sunshine coming and going, and the shadows of the clouds running races across the blank plain.

By-and-by he began to learn lessons—not that his nurse had been ordered to teach him, but she did it partly to amuse herself. She was not a stupid woman, and Prince Dolor was by no means a stupid boy; so they got on very well, and his continual entreaty "What can I do? what can you find me to do?" was stopped; at least for an hour or two in the day.

It was a dull life, but he had never known any other; anyhow, he remembered no other; and he did not pity himself at all. Not for a long time, till he grew to be quite a big little boy, and could read easily. Then he suddenly took to books, which the deaf-mute brought him from time to time—books which, not being acquainted with the literature of Nomansland, I cannot describe, but no doubt they were very interesting; and they informed him of everything in the outside world, and filled him with an intense longing to see it.

From this time a change came over the boy. He began to look sad and thin, and to shut himself up for hours without speaking. For his nurse hardly spoke, and whatever questions he asked beyond their ordinary daily life she never answered. She had, indeed, been forbidden, on pain of death, to tell him anything about himself, who he was, or what he might have been. He knew he was Prince Dolor, because she always ad-

dressed him as "my Prince," and "your Royal Highness," but what a Prince was he had not the least idea. He had no idea of anything in the world, except what he found in his books.

He sat one day surrounded by them, having built them up round him like a little castle wall. He had been reading them half the day, but feeling all the while that to read about things which you never can see is like hearing about a beautiful dinner while you are starving. For almost the first time in his life he grew melancholy: his hands fell on his lap; he sat gazing out of the window-slit upon the view outside—the view he had looked at every day of his life, and might look at for endless days more.

Not a very cheerful view—just the plain and the sky—but he liked it. He used to think, if he could only fly out of that window, up to the sky or down to the plain, how nice it would be! Perhaps when he died—his nurse had told him once in anger that he would never leave the tower till he died—he might be able to do this. Not that he understood much what dying meant, but it must be a change, and any change seemed to him a blessing.

"And I wish I had somebody to tell me all about it; about that and many other things; somebody that would be fond of me, like my poor white kitten."

Here the tears came into his eyes, for the boy's one friend, the one interest of his life, had been a little white kitten, which the deaf-mute, kindly smiling, once took out of his pocket and gave him—the only living creature Prince Dolor had ever seen. For four weeks it was his constant plaything and companion, till one moonlight night it took a fancy for wandering, climbed on to the parapet of the tower, dropped over and disappeared. It was not killed, he hoped, for cats have nine lives; indeed, he almost fancied he saw it pick itself up and scamper away, but he never caught sight of it more.

"Yes, I wish I had something better than a kitten—a person, a real live person, who would be fond of me and kind to me. Oh, I want somebody—dreadfully, dreadfully!"

As he spoke, there sounded behind him a slight tap-tap-tap, as of a stick or a cane, and twisting himself round, he saw— what do you think he saw?

Nothing either frightening or ugly, but still exceedingly curious. A little woman, no bigger than he might himself have been, had his legs grown like those of other children, but she was not a child—she was an old woman. Her hair was grey, and her dress was grey, and there was a grey shadow over her wherever she moved. But she had the sweetest smile, the prettiest hands, and when she spoke it was in the softest voice imaginable.

"My dear little boy,"—and dropping her cane, the only bright and rich thing about her, she laid those two tiny hands on his shoulders—"my own little boy, I could not come to you until you had said you wanted me, but now you do want me, here I am."

"And you are very welcome, madam," replied the Prince, trying to speak politely, as princes always did in books; "and I am exceedingly obliged to you. May I ask who you are? Perhaps my mother?" For he knew that little boys usually had a mother, and had occasionally wondered what had become of his own.

"No," said the visitor, with a tender, half-sad smile, putting back the hair from his forehead, and looking right into his eyes —"No, I am not your mother, though she was a dear friend of mine; and you are as like her as ever you can be."

"Will you tell her to come and see me then?"

"She cannot; but I dare say she knows all about you. And she loves you very much—and so do I; and I want to help you all I can, my poor little boy."

"Why do you call me poor?" asked Prince Dolor in surprise.

The little old woman glanced down on his legs and feet, which he did not know were different from those of other children, and then at his sweet, bright face, which, though he knew not that either, was exceedingly different from many children's faces, which are often so fretful, cross, sullen. Looking at him, instead of sighing, she smiled. "I beg your pardon, my Prince," said she.

"Yes, I am a Prince, and my name is Dolor; will you tell me yours, madam?"

The little old woman laughed like a chime of silver bells.

"I have not got a name—or rather, I have so many names that I don't know which to choose. However, it was I who gave you yours, and you will belong to me all your days. I am your godmother."

"Hurrah!" cried the little Prince; "I am glad I belong to you, for I like you very much. Will you come and play with me?"

So they sat down together, and played. By-and-by they began to talk.

"Are you very dull here?" asked the little old woman.

"Not particularly, thank you, godmother. I have plenty to eat and drink, and my lessons to do, and my books to read— lots of books."

"And you want nothing?"

"Nothing. Yes—perhaps—If you please, godmother, could you bring me just one more thing?"

"What sort of thing?"

"A little boy to play with."

The old woman looked very sad. "Just the thing, alas, which I cannot give you. My child, I cannot alter your lot in any way, but I can help you to bear it."

"Thank you. But why do you talk of bearing it? I have nothing to bear."

"My poor little man!" said the old woman in the very tenderest tone of her tender voice. "Kiss me!"

"What is kissing?" asked the wondering child.

His godmother took him in her arms and embraced him many times. By-and-by he kissed her back again—at first awkwardly and shyly, then with all the strength of his warm little heart.

"You are better to cuddle than even my white kitten, I think. Promise me that you will never go away."

"I must; but I will leave a present behind me—something as good as myself to amuse you—something that will take you wherever you want to go, and show you all that you wish to see."

"What is it?"

"A travelling-cloak."

The Prince's countenance fell. "I don't want a cloak, for I never go out. Sometimes nurse hoists me on to the roof, and carries me round by the parapet; but that is all. I can't walk, you know, as she does."

"The more reason why you should ride; and besides, this travelling-cloak——"

"Hush—she's coming!"

There sounded outside the room door a heavy step and a grumpy voice, and a rattle of plates and dishes.

"It's my nurse, and she is bringing my dinner; but I don't

want dinner at all—I only want you. Will her coming drive you away, godmother?"

"Perhaps; but only for a little. Never mind; all the bolts and bars in the world couldn't keep me out. I'd fly in at the window, or down through the chimney. Only wish for me, and I come."

"Thank you," said Prince Dolor, but almost in a whisper, for he was very uneasy at what might happen next. His nurse and his godmother—what would they say to one another? How would they look at one another? Two such different faces: one, harsh-lined, sullen, cross, and sad; the other, sweet and bright and calm as a summer evening before the dark begins.

When the door was flung open, Prince Dolor shut his eyes, trembling all over: opening them again, he saw he need fear nothing; his lovely old godmother had melted away just like the rainbow out of the sky, as he had watched it many a time. Nobody but his nurse was in the room.

"What a muddle your Royal Highness is sitting in," said she sharply. "Such a heap of untidy books; and what's this rubbish?" kicking a little bundle that lay beside them.

"Oh, nothing, nothing—give it me!" cried the Prince, and darting after it, he hid it under his pinafore, and then pushed it quickly into his pocket. Rubbish as it was, it was left in the place where she had sat, and might be something belonging to her—his dear, kind godmother, whom already he loved with all his lonely, tender, passionate heart.

It was, though he did not know this, his wonderful travelling-cloak.

CHAPTER FOUR

And what of the travelling-cloak? What sort of cloak was it, and what good did it do the Prince?

Stay, and I'll tell you all about it.

Outside it was the commonest-looking bundle imaginable— shabby and small; and the instant Prince Dolor touched it, it grew smaller still, dwindling down till he could put it in his trousers pocket, like a handkerchief rolled up into a ball. He did this at once, for fear his nurse should see it, and kept it there all day—all night, too. Till after his next morning's lessons he had no opportunity of examining his treasure.

When he did, it seemed no treasure at all; but a mere piece of cloth—circular in form, dark green in colour, that is, if it had any colour at all, being so worn and shabby, though not dirty. It had a split cut to the centre, forming a round hole for the neck—and that was all its shape; the shape, in fact, of those cloaks which in South America are called *ponchos*—very simple, but most graceful and convenient.

Prince Dolor had never seen anything like it. In spite of his disappointment he examined it curiously; spread it out on the floor, then arranged it on his shoulders. It felt very warm and comfortable; but it was so exceedingly shabby—the only shabby thing that the Prince had ever seen in his life.

"And what use will it be to me?" said he sadly. "I have no need of outdoor clothes, as I never go out. Why was this given me, I wonder? and what in the world am I to do with it? She must be a rather funny person, this dear godmother of mine."

Nevertheless, because she was his godmother, and had given him the cloak, he folded it carefully and put it away, poor and shabby as it was, hiding it in a safe corner of his toy-cupboard, which his nurse never meddled with. He did not want her to find it, or to laugh at it, or at his godmother—as he felt sure she would, if she knew all.

There it lay, and by-and-by he forgot all about it; nay, I am sorry to say, that, being but a child, and not seeing her again, he almost forgot his sweet old godmother, or thought of her only as he did of the angels or fairies that he read of in his books, and of her visit as if it had been a mere dream of the night.

There were times, certainly, when he recalled her; of early mornings like that morning when she appeared beside him, and late evenings, when the grey twilight reminded him of the colour of her hair and her pretty soft garments; above all, when, waking in the middle of the night, with the stars peering in at his window, or the moonlight shining across his little bed, he would not have been surprised to see her standing beside it, looking at him with those beautiful tender eyes, which seemed to have a pleasantness and comfort in them different from anything he had ever known.

But she never came, and gradually she slipped out of his memory—only a boy's memory, after all; until something happened which made him remember her, and want her as he had never wanted anything before.

Prince Dolor fell ill. He caught—his nurse could not tell how —a complaint common to the people of Nomansland, called the doldrums, as unpleasant as measles or any other of our complaints; and it made him restless, cross, and disagreeable. Even when a little better, he was too weak to enjoy anything, but lay all day long on his sofa, fidgeting his nurse extremely— while, in her intense terror lest he might die, she fidgeted him still more. At last, seeing he really was getting well, she left him to himself—which he was most glad of, in spite of his dulness and dreariness. There he lay, alone, quite alone.

Now and then an irritable fit came over him, in which he longed to get up and do something, or go somewhere—would have liked to imitate his white kitten—jump down from the tower and run away, taking the chance of whatever might happen.

Only one thing, alas! was likely to happen; for the kitten, he remembered, had four active legs, while he——

"I wonder what my godmother meant when she looked at my legs and sighed so bitterly? I wonder why I can't walk straight and steady like my nurse—only I wouldn't like to have her great noisy, clumping shoes. Still, it would be very nice to move about quickly—perhaps to fly, like a bird, like that string of birds I saw the other day skimming across the sky—one after the other."

These were the passage-birds—the only living creatures that ever crossed the lonely plain; and he had been much interested in them, wondering whence they came and whither they were going.

"How nice it must be to be a bird. If legs are no good, why cannot one have wings? People have wings when they die— perhaps: I wish I was dead, that I do. I am so tired, so tired; and nobody cares for me. Nobody ever did care for me, except perhaps my godmother. Godmother, dear, have you quite forsaken me?"

He stretched himself wearily, gathered himself up, and

dropped his head upon his hands; as he did so, he felt somebody kiss him at the back of his neck, and turning, found that he was resting, not on the sofa-pillows, but on a warm shoulder—that of the little old woman clothed in grey.

How glad he was to see her! How he looked into her kind eyes, and felt her hands, to see if she were all real and alive! Then put both his arms round her neck, and kissed her as if he would never have done kissing!

"Stop, stop!" cried she, pretending to be smothered. "I see you have not forgotten my teachings. Kissing is a good thing —in moderation. Only, just let me have breath to speak one word."

"A dozen!" he said.

"Well, then, tell me all that has happened to you since I saw you—or rather, since you saw me, which is a quite different thing."

"Nothing has happened—nothing ever does happen to me," answered the Prince dolefully.

"And are you very dull, my boy?"

"So dull, that I was just thinking whether I could not jump down to the bottom of the tower like my white kitten."

"Don't do that, being not a white kitten."

"I wish I were!—I wish I were anything but what I am!"

"And you can't make yourself any different, nor can I do it either. You must be content to stay just what you are."

The little old woman said this—very firmly, but gently, too —with her arms round his neck and her lips on his forehead. It was the first time the boy had ever heard anyone talk like this, and he looked up in surprise—but not in pain, for her sweet manner softened the hardness of her words.

"Now, my Prince—for you are a Prince, and must behave as

such—let us see what we can do; how much I can do for you, or show you how to do for yourself. Where is your travelling-cloak?"

Prince Dolor blushed extremely. "I—I put it away in the cupboard; I suppose it is there still."

"You have never used it; you dislike it?"

He hesitated, not wishing to be impolite. "Don't you think it's—just a little old and shabby, for a Prince?"

The old woman laughed—long and loud, though very sweetly.

"Prince, indeed! Why, if all the princes in the world craved for it, they couldn't get it, unless I gave it them. Old and shabby! It's the most valuable thing imaginable! Very few ever have it; but I thought I would give it to you, because—because you are different from other people."

"Am I?" said the Prince, and looked first with curiosity, then with a sort of anxiety, into his godmother's face, which was sad and grave, with slow tears beginning to steal down.

She touched his poor little legs. "These are not like those of other little boys."

"Indeed!—my nurse never told me that."

"Very likely not. But it is time you were told; and I tell you, because I love you."

"Tell me what, dear godmother?"

"That you will never be able to walk, or run, or jump, or play—that your life will be quite different to most people's lives: but it may be a happy life for all that. Do not be afraid."

"I am not afraid," said the boy; but he turned very pale, and his lips began to quiver, though he did not actually cry—he was too old for that, and, perhaps, too proud.

Though not wholly comprehending, he began dimly to guess what his godmother meant. He had never seen any real live boys, but he had seen pictures of them; running and jumping; which he had admired and tried hard to imitate, but always failed. Now he began to understand why he failed, and that he always should fail—that, in fact, he was not like other little boys; and it was of no use his wishing to do as they did, and play as they played, even if he had had them to play with. His was a separate life, in which he must find out new work and new pleasures for himself.

The sense of *the inevitable*, as grown-up people call it—that we cannot have things as we want them to be, but as they are, and that we must learn to bear them and make the best of them —this lesson, which everybody has to learn soon or late—came, alas! sadly soon, to the poor boy. He fought against it for a while, and then, quite overcome, turned and sobbed bitterly in his godmother's arms.

She comforted him—I do not know how, except that love always comforts; and then she whispered to him, in her sweet, strong, cheerful voice—"Never mind!"

"No, I don't think I do mind—that is, I *won't* mind," replied he, catching the courage of her tone and speaking like a man, though he was still such a mere boy.

"That is right, my Prince!—that is being like a Prince. Now we know exactly where we are; let us put our shoulders to the wheel and——"

"We are in Hopeless Tower" (this was its name, if it had a name), "and there is no wheel to put our shoulders to," said the child sadly.

"You little matter-of-fact goose! Well for you that you have a godmother called——"

"What?" he eagerly asked.

"Stuff-and-nonsense."

"Stuff-and-nonsense! What a funny name!"

"Some people give it me, but they are not my most intimate friends. These call me—never mind what," added the old woman, with a soft twinkle in her eyes. "So as you know me, and know me well, you may give me any name you please; it doesn't matter. But I am your godmother, child. I have few godchildren; those I have love me dearly, and find me the greatest blessing in all the world."

"I can well believe it," cried the little lame Prince, and forgot his troubles in looking at her—as her figure dilated, her eyes grew lustrous as stars, her very raiment brightened, and the whole room seemed filled with her beautiful and beneficent presence like light.

He could have looked at her for ever—half in love, half in awe; but she suddenly dwindled down into the little old woman all in grey, and with a malicious twinkle in her eyes, asked for the travelling-cloak.

"Bring it out of the rubbish cupboard, and shake the dust off it, quick!" said she to Prince Dolor, who hung his head, rather ashamed. "Spread it out on the floor, and wait till the split closes and the edges turn up like a rim all round. Then go and open the skylight—mind, I say *open the skylight*—set yourself down in the middle of it, like a frog on a water-lily leaf; say 'Abracadabra, dum dum dum,' and—see what will happen!"

The Prince burst into a fit of laughing. It all seemed so exceedingly silly; he wondered that a wise old woman like his godmother should talk such nonsense.

"Stuff-and-nonsense, you mean," said she, answering, to his great alarm, his unspoken thoughts. "Did I not tell you some people called me by that name? Never mind; it doesn't harm me."

And she laughed—her merry laugh—as childlike as if she were the Prince's age instead of her own, whatever that might be. She certainly was a most extraordinary old woman.

"Believe me or not, it doesn't matter," said she. "Here is the cloak: when you want to go travelling on it, say *Abracadabra, dum dum dum*; when you want to come back again, say *Abracadabra, tum tum ti*. That's all; good-bye."

A puff of pleasant air passing by him, and making him feel for the moment quite strong and well, was all the Prince was conscious of. His most extraordinary godmother was gone.

"Really now, how rosy your Royal Highness's cheeks have grown! You seem to have got well already," said the nurse, entering the room.

"I think I have," replied the Prince very gently—he felt kindly and gently even to his grim nurse. "And now let me have my dinner, and go you to your sewing as usual."

The instant she was gone, however, taking with her the plates and dishes, which for the first time since his illness he had satisfactorily cleared, Prince Dolor sprang down from his sofa, and with one or two of his frog-like jumps, not graceful but convenient, he reached the cupboard where he kept his toys, and looked everywhere for his travelling-cloak.

Alas! it was not there.

While he was ill of the doldrums, his nurse, thinking it a good opportunity for putting things to rights, had made a grand clearance of all his "rubbish," as she considered it: his beloved headless horses, broken carts, sheep without feet, and birds without wings—all the treasures of his baby days, which he could not bear to part with. Though he seldom played with them now, he liked just to feel they were there.

They were all gone! and with them the travelling-cloak. He

sat down on the floor, looking at the empty shelves, so beautifully clean and tidy, then burst out sobbing as if his heart would break.

But quietly—always quietly. He never let his nurse hear him cry. She only laughed at him, as he felt she would laugh now.

"And it is all my own fault," he cried. "I ought to have taken better care of my godmother's gift. O, godmother, forgive me! I'll never be so careless again. I don't know what the cloak is exactly, but I am sure it is something precious. Help me to find it again. Oh, don't let it be stolen from me—don't, please!"

"Ha, ha, ha!" laughed a silvery voice. "Why, that travelling-cloak is the one thing in the world which nobody can steal. It is of no use to anybody except the owner. Open your eyes, my Prince, and see what you shall see."

His dear old godmother, he thought, and turned eagerly round. But no; he only beheld, lying in a corner of the room, all dust and cobwebs, his precious travelling-cloak.

Prince Dolor darted towards it, tumbling several times on the way—as he often did tumble, poor boy! and pick himself up again, never complaining. Snatching it to his breast, he hugged and kissed it, cobwebs and all, as if it had been something alive. Then he began unrolling it, wondering each minute what would happen. But what did happen was so curious that I must leave it for another chapter.

CHAPTER FIVE

If any reader, big or little, should wonder whether there is a meaning in this story, deeper than that of an ordinary fairy tale, I will own that there is. But I have hidden it so carefully that the smaller people, and many larger folk, will never find it out, and meantime the book may be read straight on, like "Cinderella," or "Blue-Beard," or "Hop-o'-my Thumb," for what interest it has, or what amusement it may bring.

Having said this, I return to Prince Dolor, that little lame boy whom many may think so exceedingly to be pitied. But if you had seen him as he sat patiently untying his wonderful cloak, which was done up in a very tight and perplexing parcel, using skilfully his deft little hands, and knitting his brows with firm determination, while his eyes glistened with pleasure, and energy, and eager anticipation—if you had beheld him thus, you might have changed your opinion.

When we see people suffering or unfortunate, we feel very sorry for them; but when we see them bravely bearing their sufferings, and making the best of their misfortunes, it is quite a different feeling. We respect, we admire them. One can respect and admire even a little child.

When Prince Dolor had patiently untied all the knots, a remarkable thing happened. The cloak began to undo itself. Slowly unfolding, it laid itself down on the carpet, as flat as if it had been ironed; the split joined with a little sharp crick-crack, and the rim turned up all round till it was breast-high;

for meantime the cloak had grown and grown, and become quite large enough for one person to sit in it, as comfortable as if in a boat.

The Prince watched it rather anxiously; it was such an extraordinary, not to say a frightening thing. However, he was no coward, but a thorough boy, who, if he had been like other boys, would doubtless have grown up daring and adventurous —a soldier, a sailor, or the like. As it was, he could only show his courage morally, not physically, by being afraid of nothing, and by doing boldly all that it was in his narrow powers to do. And I am not sure but that in this way he showed more real valour than if he had had six pairs of proper legs.

He said to himself, "What a goose I am! As if my dear godmother would ever have given me anything to hurt me. Here goes!"

So, with one of his active leaps, he sprang right into the middle of the cloak, where he squatted down, wrapping his arms tight round his knees, for they shook a little and his heart beat fast. But there he sat, steady and silent, waiting for what might happen next.

Nothing did happen, and he began to think nothing would, and to feel rather disappointed, when he recollected the words he had been told to repeat—"Abracadabra, dum, dum, dum!"

He repeated them, laughing all the while, they seemed such nonsense. And then—and then——

Now, I don't expect anybody to believe what I am going to relate, though a good many wise people have believed a good many sillier things. And as seeing's believing, and I never saw it, I cannot be expected implicitly to believe it myself, except in a sort of a way; and yet there is truth in it—for some people.

The cloak rose, slowly and steadily, at first only a few inches, then gradually higher and higher, till it nearly touched the sky-light. Prince Dolor's head actually bumped against the glass, or would have done so, had he not crouched down, crying, "Oh, please don't hurt me!" in a most melancholy voice.

Then he suddenly remembered his godmother's express command—"Open the skylight!"

Regaining his courage at once, without a moment's delay, he lifted up his head and began searching for the bolt, the cloak meanwhile remaining perfectly still, balanced in air. But the minute the window was opened, out it sailed—right out into the clear fresh air, with nothing between it and the cloudless blue.

Prince Dolor had never felt any such delicious sensation before! I can understand it. Cannot you? Did you never think, in watching the rooks going home singly or in pairs, oaring their way across the calm evening sky, till they vanish like black dots in the misty grey, how pleasant it must feel to be up there, quite out of the noise and din of the world, able to hear and see everything down below, yet troubled by nothing and teased by no one—all alone, but perfectly content.

Something like this was the happiness of the little lame Prince when he got out of Hopeless Tower, and found himself for the first time in the pure open air, with the sky above him and the earth below.

True, there was nothing but earth and sky; no houses, no trees, no rivers, mountains, seas—not a beast on the ground, or a bird in the air. But to him even the level plain looked beautiful; and then there was the glorious arch of the sky, with a little young moon sitting in the west like a baby queen. And the evening breeze was so sweet and fresh, it kissed him like his godmother's kisses; and by-and-by a few stars came out, first two or three, and then quantities—quantities! so that, when he began to count them, he was utterly bewildered.

By this time, however, the cool breeze had become cold, the mist gathered, and as he had, as he said, no outdoor clothes, poor Prince Dolor was not very comfortable. The dews fell damp on his curls—he began to shiver.

"Perhaps I had better go home," thought he.

But how?—For in his excitement the other words which his godmother had told him to use had slipped his memory. They were only a little different from the first, but in that slight difference all the importance lay. As he repeated his "Abracadabra," trying ever so many other syllables after it, the cloak only went faster and faster, skimming on through the dusky empty air.

The poor little Prince began to feel frightened. What if his wonderful travelling-cloak should keep on thus travelling, perhaps to the world's end, carrying with it a poor, tired, hungry boy, who, after all, was beginning to think there was something very pleasant in supper and bed?

"Dear godmother," he cried pitifully, "do help me! Tell me just this once and I'll never forget again."

Instantly the words came rushing into his head—"Abracadabra, tum, tum, ti!" Was that it? Ah, yes!—for the cloak began to turn slowly. He repeated the charm again, more distinctly and firmly, when it gave a gentle dip, like a nod of satisfaction, and immediately started back, as fast as ever, in the direction of the tower.

He reached the skylight, which he found exactly as he had left it, and slipped in, cloak and all, as easily as he had got out. He had scarcely reached the floor, and was still sitting in the middle of his travelling-cloak—like a frog on a water-lily leaf, as his godmother had expressed it—when he heard his nurse's voice outside.

"Bless us! what has become of your Royal Highness all this time? To sit stupidly here at the window till it is quite dark, and leave the skylight open too. Prince! What can you be thinking of? You are the silliest boy I ever knew."

"Am I?" said he absently, and never heeding her crossness; for his only anxiety was lest she might find out anything.

She would have been a very clever person to have done so. The instant Prince Dolor got off it, the cloak folded itself up into the tiniest possible parcel, tied all its own knots, and rolled itself of its own accord into the farthest and darkest corner of the room. If the nurse had seen it, which she didn't, she would have taken it for a mere bundle of rubbish not worth noticing.

Shutting the skylight with an angry bang, she brought in the supper and lit the candles, with her usual unhappy expression of countenance. But Prince Dolor hardly saw it; he only saw, hid in the corner where nobody else would see it, his wonderful travelling-cloak. And though his supper was not particularly nice, he ate it heartily, scarcely hearing a word of his nurse's grumbling, which to-night seemed to have taken the place of her sullen silence.

"Poor woman!" he thought, when he paused a minute to listen and look at her, with those quiet, happy eyes, so like his mother's. "Poor woman! *she* hasn't got a travelling-cloak!"

And when he was left alone at last, and crept into his little bed, where he lay awake a good while, watching what he called his "sky-garden," all planted with stars, like flowers, his chief thought was, "I must be up very early to-morrow morning and get my lessons done, and then I'll go travelling all over the world on my beautiful cloak."

So, next day, he opened his eyes with the sun, and went with a good heart to his lessons. They had hitherto been the chief amusement of his dull life; now, I am afraid, he found them also a little dull. But he tried to be good—I don't say Prince Dolor always was good, but he generally tried to be—and when his mind went wandering after the dark dusty corner where lay his precious treasure, he resolutely called it back again.

"For," he said, "how ashamed my godmother would be of me if I grew up a stupid boy."

But the instant lessons were done, and he was alone in the empty room, he crept across the floor, undid the shabby little bundle, his fingers trembling with eagerness, climbed on the chair, and thence to the table, so as to unbar the skylight— he forgot nothing now—said his magic charm, and was away out of the window, as children say, "in a few minutes less than no time!"

Nobody missed him. He was accustomed to sit so quietly always, that his nurse, though only in the next room, perceived no difference. And besides, she might have gone in and out a dozen times, and it would have been just the same; she never could have found out his absence.

For what do you think the clever godmother did? She took a quantity of moonshine, or some equally convenient material, and made an image, which she set on the window-sill reading, or by the table drawing, where it looked so like Prince Dolor, that any common observer would never have guessed the deception; and even the boy would have been puzzled to know which was the image and which was himself.

And all this while the happy little fellow was away, floating in the air on his magic cloak, and seeing all sorts of wonderful things—or they seemed wonderful to him, who had hitherto seen nothing at all.

First, there were the flowers that grew on the plain, which, whenever the cloak came near enough, he strained his eyes to look at; they were very tiny, but very beautiful—white saxifrage, and yellow lotus, and ground-thistles, purple and bright, with many others the names of which I do not know. No more did Prince Dolor, though he tried to find them out by recalling any pictures he had seen of them. But he was too far off; and though it was pleasant enough to admire them as brilliant patches of colour, still he would have liked to examine them all. He was, as a little girl I know once said of a playfellow, "a very *examining* boy."

"I wonder," he thought, "whether I could see better through a pair of glasses like those my nurse reads with, and takes such care of. How I would take care of them too, if only I had a pair!"

Immediately he felt something queer and hard fixing itself on to the bridge of his nose. It was a pair of the prettiest gold spectacles ever seen; and looking downwards, he found that, though ever so high above the ground, he could see every minute blade of grass, every tiny bud and flower—nay, even the insects that walked over them.

"Thank you, thank you!" he cried in a gush of gratitude—to anybody or everybody, but especially to his dear godmother, whom he felt sure had given him this new present. He amused himself with it for ever so long, with his chin pressed on the rim of the cloak, gazing down upon the grass, every square foot of which was a mine of wonders.

Then, just to rest his eyes, he turned them up to the sky—the blue, bright, empty sky, which he had looked at so often and seen nothing.

Now, surely there was something. A long, black, wavy line, moving on in the distance, not by chance, as the clouds move apparently, but deliberately, as if it were alive. He might have seen it before—he almost thought he had; but then he could not tell what it was. Looking at it through his spectacles, he discovered that it really was alive; being a long string of birds, flying one after the other, their wings moving steadily and their heads pointed in one direction, as steadily as if each were a little ship, guided invisibly by an unerring helm.

"They must be the passage-birds flying seawards!" cried the boy, who had read a little about them, and had a great talent for putting two and two together and finding out all he could. "Oh, how I should like to see them quite close, and to know where they come from, and whither they are going! How I wish I knew everything in all the world!"

A silly speech for even an "examining" little boy to make; because, as we grow older, the more we know, the more we find out there is to know. And Prince Dolor blushed when he had said it, and hoped nobody had heard him.

Apparently somebody had, however; for the cloak gave a sudden bound forward, and presently he found himself high up in air, in the very middle of that band of aerial travellers, who had no magic cloak to travel on—nothing except their wings. Yet there they were, making their fearless way through the sky.

Prince Dolor looked at them, as one after the other they glided past him; and they looked at him—those pretty swallows, with their changing necks and bright eyes—as if wondering to meet in mid-air such an extraordinary sort of a bird.

"Oh, I wish I were going with you, you lovely creatures!" cried the boy. "I'm getting so tired of this dull plain, and the dreary and lonely tower. I do so want to see the world! Pretty swallows, dear swallows! Tell me what it looks like—the beautiful, wonderful world!"

But the swallows flew past him—steadily, slowly, pursuing their course as if inside each little head had been a mariner's compass, to guide them safe over land and sea, direct to the place where they desired to go.

The boy looked after them with envy. For a long time he followed with his eyes the faint wavy black line as it floated away, sometimes changing its curves a little, but never deviating from its settled course, till it vanished entirely out of sight.

Then he settled himself down in the centre of the cloak, feeling quite sad and lonely.

"I think I'll go home," said he, and repeated his "Abracadabra, tum, tum, ti!" with a rather heavy heart. The more he had, the more he wanted; and it is not always one can have everything one wants—at least, at the exact minute one craves for it; not even though one is a Prince, and has a powerful and beneficent godmother.

He did not like to vex her by calling for her, and telling her how unhappy he was, in spite of all her goodness; so he just kept his trouble to himself, went back to his lonely tower, and spent three days in silent melancholy without even attempting another journey on his travelling-cloak.

CHAPTER SIX

The fourth day it happened that the deaf-mute paid his accustomed visit, after which Prince Dolor's spirits rose. They always did, when he got the new books, which, just to relieve his conscience, the King of Nomansland regularly sent to his nephew; with many new toys also, though the latter were disregarded now.

"Toys indeed! when I'm a big boy," said the Prince with disdain, and would scarcely condescend to mount a rocking-horse, which had come, somehow or other—I can't be expected to explain things very exactly—packed on the back of the other, the great black horse, which stood and fed contentedly at the bottom of the tower.

Prince Dolor leaned over and looked at it, and thought how grand it must be to get upon its back—this grand live steed—and ride away, like the pictures of knights.

"Suppose I was a knight," he said to himself; "then I should be obliged to ride out and see the world."

But he kept all these thoughts to himself, and just sat still, devouring his new books till he had come to the end of them all. It was a repast not unlike the Barmecide's feast which you read of in the "Arabian Nights," which consisted of very elegant but empty dishes, or that supper of Sancho Panza in "Don Quixote," where, the minute the smoking dishes came on the table, the physician waved his hand and they were all taken away.

Thus, almost all the ordinary delights of boy-life had been taken away from, or rather never given to, this poor little Prince.

"I wonder," he would sometimes think—"I wonder what it feels like to be on the back of a horse, galloping away, or holding the reins in a carriage, and tearing across the country, or jumping a ditch, or running a race, such as I read of or see in pictures. What a lot of things there are that I should like to do! But first, I should like to go and see the world. I'll try."

Apparently it was his godmother's plan always to let him try, and try hard, before he gained anything. This day the knots that tied up his travelling-cloak were more than usually troublesome, and he was a full half hour before he got out into the open air, and found himself floating merrily over the top of the tower.

Hitherto, in all his journeys he had never let himself go out of sight of home, for the dreary building, after all, was home —he remembered no other; but now he felt sick of the very look of his tower, with its round smooth walls and level battlements.

"Off we go!" cried he, when the cloak stirred itself with a slight slow motion, as if waiting his orders. "Anywhere—anywhere, so that I am away from here, and out into the world."

As he spoke, the cloak, as if seized suddenly with a new idea, bounded forward and went skimming through the air, faster than the very fastest railway train.

"Gee-up, gee-up!" cried Prince Dolor in great excitement. "This is as good as riding a race."

And he patted the cloak as if it had been a horse—that is, in the way he supposed horses ought to be patted; and tossed his head back to meet the fresh breeze, and pulled his coat-collar up and his hat down, as he felt the wind grow keener and colder, colder than anything he had ever known.

"What does it matter though?" said he. "I'm a boy, and boys ought not to mind anything."

Still, for all his good-will, by-and-by he began to shiver exceedingly; also, he had come away without his dinner, and he grew frightfully hungry. And to add to everything, the sunshiny day changed into rain, and being high up, in the very midst of the clouds, he got soaked through and through in a very few minutes.

"Shall I turn back?" meditated he. "Suppose I say 'Abracadabra?'"

Here he stopped, for already the cloak gave an obedient lurch, as if it were expecting to be sent home immediately.

"No—I can't—I can't go back! I must go forward and see the world. But oh! if I had but the shabbiest old rug to shelter me from the rain, or the driest morsel of bread and cheese, just to keep me from starving! Still, I don't much mind; I'm a Prince, and ought to be able to stand anything. Hold on, cloak, we'll make the best of it."

It was a most curious circumstance, but no sooner had he said this than he felt stealing over his knees something warm and soft; in fact, a most beautiful bearskin, which folded itself round him quite naturally, and cuddled him up as closely as if he had been the cub of the kind old mother bear that once owned it. Then feeling in his pocket, which suddenly stuck out in a marvellous way, he found, not exactly bread and cheese, nor even sandwiches, but a packet of the most delicious food he had ever tasted. It was not meat, nor pudding, but a combination of both, and it served him excellently for both. He ate his dinner with the greatest gusto imaginable, till he grew so thirsty he did not know what to do.

"Couldn't I have just one drop of water, if it didn't trouble you too much, kindest of godmothers."

For he really thought this want was beyond her power to supply. All the water which supplied Hopeless Tower was pumped up with difficulty, from a deep artesian well—there were such things known in Nomansland—which had been made at the foot of it. But around, for miles upon miles, the desolate plain was perfectly dry. And above it, high in air, how could he expect to find a well, or to get even a drop of water?

He forgot one thing—the rain. While he spoke, it came on in another wild burst, as if the clouds had poured themselves out in a passion of crying, wetting him certainly, but leaving behind, in a large glass vessel which he had never noticed before, enough water to quench the thirst of two or three boys at least. And it was so fresh, so pure—as water from the clouds always is, when it does not catch the soot from city chimneys and other defilements—that he drank it, every drop, with the greatest delight and content.

Also, as soon as it was empty, the rain filled it again, so that he was able to wash his face and hands and refresh himself exceedingly. Then the sun came out and dried him in no time. After that he curled himself up under the bearskin rug, and though he determined to be the most wide-awake boy imaginable, being so exceedingly snug and warm and comfortable, Prince Dolor condescended to shut his eyes, just for one minute. The next minute he was sound asleep.

When he awoke, he found himself floating over a country quite unlike anything he had ever seen before.

Yet it was nothing but what most of you children see every day and never notice it—a pretty country landscape, like England, Scotland, France, or any other land you choose to name.

It had no particular features—nothing in it grand or lovely— was simply pretty, nothing more; yet to Prince Dolor, who had never gone beyond his lonely tower and level plain, it appeared the most charming sight imaginable.

First, there was a river. It came tumbling down the hillside, frothing and foaming, playing at hide-and-seek among rocks, then bursting out in noisy fun like a child, to bury itself in deep still pools. Afterwards it went steadily on for a while, like a good grown-up person, till it came to another big rock, where it misbehaved itself extremely. It turned into a cataract and went tumbling over and over, after a fashion that made the Prince —who had never seen water before, except in his bath or his drinking-cup—clap his hands with delight.

"It is so active, so alive! I like things active and alive!" cried he, and watched it shimmering and dancing, whirling and leaping, till, after a few windings and vagaries, it settled into a respectable stream. After that it went along, deep and quiet, but flowing steadily on, till it reached a large lake, into which it slipped, and so ended its course.

All this the boy saw, either with his own naked eye, or through his gold spectacles. He saw also as in a picture, beautiful but silent, many other things, which struck him with wonder, especially a grove of trees.

Only think, to have lived to his age (which he himself did not know, as he did not know his own birthday) and never to have seen trees! As he floated over these oaks, they seemed to him—trunk, branches, and leaves—the most curious sight imaginable.

"If I could only get nearer, so as to touch them," said he, and immediately the obedient cloak ducked down; Prince Dolor made a snatch at the topmost twig of the tallest tree, and caught a bunch of leaves in his hand.

Just a bunch of green leaves—such as we see in myriads; watching them bud, grow, fall, and then kicking them along on the ground as if they were worth nothing. Yet, how wonderful they are—every one of them a little different. I don't suppose you could ever find two leaves exactly alike, in form, colour, and size—no more than you could find two faces alike, or two characters exactly the same. The plan of this world is infinite similarity and yet infinite variety.

Prince Dolor examined his leaves with the greatest curiosity —and also a little caterpillar that he found walking over one of them. He coaxed it to take an additional walk over his finger, which it did with the greatest dignity and decorum, as if it, Mr. Caterpillar, were the most important individual in existence. It amused him for a long time; and when a sudden gust of wind blew it overboard, leaves and all, he felt quite disconsolate.

"Still, there must be many live creatures in the world besides caterpillars. I should like to see a few of them."

The cloak gave a little dip down, as if to say "All right, my Prince," and bore him across the oak forest to a long fertile valley—called in Scotland a strath, and in England a weald— but what they call it in the tongue of Nomansland I do not know. It was made up of cornfields, pasturefields, lanes, hedges, brooks, and ponds. Also, in it were what the Prince had desired to see, a quantity of living creatures, wild and tame. Cows and horses, lambs and sheep, fed in the meadows; pigs and fowls walked about the farmyards; and, in lonelier places, hares scudded, rabbits burrowed, and pheasants and partridges, with many other smaller birds, inhabited the fields and woods.

Through his wonderful spectacles the Prince could see everything; but, as I said, it was a silent picture; he was too high up to catch anything except a faint murmur, which only aroused his anxiety to hear more.

"I have as good as two pairs of eyes," he thought. "I wonder if my godmother would give me a second pair of ears."

Scarcely had he spoken, than he found lying on his lap the most curious little parcel, all done up in silvery paper. And it contained—what do you think? Actually, a pair of silver ears, which, when he tried them on, fitted so exactly over his own, that he hardly felt them, except for the difference they made in his hearing.

There is something which we listen to daily and never notice. I mean the sounds of the visible world, animate and inanimate. Winds blowing, waters flowing, trees stirring, insects whirring (dear me! I am quite unconsciously writing rhyme), with the various cries of birds and beasts—lowing cattle, bleating sheep, grunting pigs, and cackling hens—all the infinite discords that somehow or other make a beautiful harmony.

We hear this, and are so accustomed to it that we think nothing of it; but Prince Dolor, who had lived all his days in the dead silence of Hopeless Tower, heard it for the first time. And oh! if you had seen his face.

He listened, listened, as if he could never have done listening. And he looked and looked, as if he could not gaze enough. Above all, the motion of the animals delighted him: cows walking, horses galloping, little lambs and calves running races across the meadows, were such a treat for him to watch—he that was always so quiet. But, these creatures having four legs, and he only two, the difference did not strike him painfully.

Still, by-and-by, after the fashion of children—and, I fear, of many big people too—he began to want something more than he had, something that would be quite fresh and new.

"Godmother," he said, having now begun to believe that, whether he saw her or not, he could always speak to her with full confidence that she would hear him—"Godmother, all these creatures I like exceedingly—but I should like better to see a creature like myself. Couldn't you show me just one little boy?"

There was a sigh behind him—it might have been only the wind—and the cloak remained so long balanced motionless in air, that he was half afraid his godmother had forgotten him, or was offended with him for asking too much. Suddenly, a shrill whistle startled him, even through his silver ears, and looking downwards, he saw start up from behind a bush on a common, something—

Neither a sheep, nor a horse, nor a cow—nothing upon four legs. This creature had only two; but they were long, straight, and strong. And it had a lithe active body, and a curly head of black hair set upon its shoulders. It was a boy, a shepherdboy, about the Prince's own age—but, oh! so different.

Not that he was an ugly boy—though his face was almost as red as his hands, and his shaggy hair matted like the backs of his own sheep. He was rather a nice-looking lad; and seemed so bright, and healthy, and good-tempered—"jolly" would be the word, only I am not sure if they have such an one in the elegant language of Nomansland—that the little Prince watched him with great admiration.

"Might he come and play with me? I would drop down to the ground to him, or fetch him up to me here. Oh, how nice it would be if I only had a little boy to play with me!"

But the cloak, usually so obedient to his wishes, disobeyed

him now. There were evidently some things which his god-mother either could not or would not give. The cloak hung stationary, high in air, never attempting to descend. The shep-herdlad evidently took it for a large bird, and shading his eyes, looked up at it, making the Prince's heart beat fast.

However, nothing ensued. The boy turned round, with a long, loud whistle—seemingly his usual and only way of express-ing his feelings. He could not make the thing out exactly—it was a rather mysterious affair, but it did not trouble him much—*he* was not an "examining" boy.

Then, stretching himself, for he had been evidently half asleep, he began flopping his shoulders with his arms, to wake and warm himself; while his dog, a rough collie, who had been guarding the sheep meanwhile, began to jump upon him, bark-ing with delight.

"Down Snap, down! Stop that, or I'll thrash you," the Prince heard him say; though with such a rough hard voice and queer pronunciation that it was difficult to make the words out. "Hollo! Let's warm ourselves by a race."

They started off together, boy and dog—barking and shout-ing, till it was doubtful which made the most noise or ran the fastest. A regular steeplechase it was: first across the level com-mon, greatly disturbing the quiet sheep; and then tearing away across country, scrambling through hedges, and leaping ditches, and tumbling up and down over ploughed fields. They did not seem to have anything to run for—but as if they did it, both of them, for the mere pleasure of motion.

And what a pleasure that seemed! To the dog of course, but scarcely less so to the boy. How he skimmed along over the ground—his cheeks glowing, and his hair flying, and his legs —oh, what a pair of legs he had!

Prince Dolor watched him with great intentness, and in a state of excitement almost equal to that of the runner himself —for a while. Then the sweet pale face grew a trifle paler, the lips began to quiver and the eyes to fill.

"How nice it must be to run like that!" he said softly, thinking that never—no, never in this world—would he be able to do the same.

Now he understood what his godmother had meant when she gave him his travelling-cloak, and why he had heard that sigh—he was sure it was hers—when he had asked to see "just one little boy."

"I think I had rather not look at him again," said the poor little Prince, drawing himself back into the centre of his cloak, and resuming his favourite posture, sitting like a Turk, with his arms wrapped round his feeble, useless legs.

"You're no good to me," he said, patting them mournfully. "You never will be any good to me. I wonder why I had you at all; I wonder why I was born at all, since I was not to grow up like other little boys. *Why* not?"

A question, so strange, so sad, yet so often occurring in some form or other, in this world—as you will find, my children, when you are older—that even if he had put it to his mother she could only have answered it, as we have to answer many as difficult things, by simply saying "I don't know." There is much that we do not know, and cannot understand—we big folks, no more than you little ones. We have to accept it all just as you have to accept anything which your parents may tell you, even though you don't as yet see the reason of it. You may some time, if you do exactly as they tell you, and are content to wait.

Prince Dolor sat a good while thus, or it appeared to him a

good while, so many thoughts came and went through his poor young mind—thoughts of great bitterness, which, little though he was, seemed to make him grow years older in a few minutes.

Then he fancied the cloak began to rock gently to and fro, with a soothing kind of motion, as if he were in somebody's arms: somebody who did not speak, but loved him and comforted him without need of words; not by deceiving him with false encouragement or hope, but by making him see the plain hard truth, in all its hardness, and thus letting him quietly face it, till it grew softened down, and did not seem nearly so dreadful after all.

Through the dreary silence and blankness, for he had placed himself so that he could see nothing but the sky, and had taken off his silver ears, as well as his gold spectacles—what was the use of either when he had no legs to walk or run?—up from below there rose a delicious sound.

You have heard it hundreds of times, my children, and so have I. When I was a child I thought there was nothing so sweet; and I think so still. It was just the song of a skylark, mounting higher and higher from the ground, till it came so close that Prince Dolor could distinguish its quivering wings and tiny body, almost too tiny to contain such a gush of music.

"O, you beautiful, beautiful bird!" cried he. "I should dearly like to take you in and cuddle you. That is, if I could—if I dared."

But he hesitated. The little brown creature with its loud heavenly voice almost made him afraid. Nevertheless, it also made him happy; and he watched and listened—so absorbed that he forgot all regret and pain, forgot everything in the world except the little lark.

It soared and soared, and he was just wondering if it would

soar out of sight, and what in the world he should do when it was gone, when it suddenly closed its wings, as larks do, when they mean to drop to the ground. But, instead of dropping to the ground, it dropped right into the little boy's breast.

What felicity! If it would only stay! A tiny soft thing to fondle and kiss, to sing to him all day long, and be his playfellow and companion, tame and tender, while to the rest of the world it was a wild bird of the air. What a pride, what a delight! To have something that nobody else had—something all his own. As the travelling-cloak travelled on, he little heeded where, and the lark still stayed, nestled down in his bosom, hopped from his hand to his shoulder, and kissed him with its dainty beak, as if it loved him, Prince Dolor forgot all his grief, and was entirely happy.

But when he got in sight of Hopeless Tower, a painful thought struck him.

"My pretty bird, what am I to do with you? If I take you into my room and shut you up there, you, a wild skylark of the air, what will become of you? I am used to this, but you are not. You will be so miserable, and suppose my nurse should find you—she who can't bear the sound of singing? Besides, I remember her once telling me that the nicest thing she ever ate in her life was lark pie!"

The little boy shivered all over at the thought. And, though the merry lark immediately broke into the loudest carol, as if saying derisively that he defied anybody to eat *him*—still Prince Dolor was very uneasy. In another minute he had made up his mind.

"No, my bird, nothing so dreadful shall happen to you if I can help it; I would rather do without you altogether. Yes, I'll try. Fly away, my darling, my beautiful! Good-bye, my merry, merry bird."

Opening his two caressing hands, in which, as if for protection, he had folded it, he let the lark go. It lingered a minute, perching on the rim of the cloak, and looking at him with eyes of almost human tenderness; then away it flew, far up into the blue sky. It was only a bird.

But, some time after, when Prince Dolor had eaten his supper—somewhat drearily, except for the thought that he could not possibly sup off lark pie now—and gone quietly to bed, the old familiar little bed, where he was accustomed to sleep, or lie awake contentedly thinking—suddenly he heard outside the window a little faint carol—faint but cheerful—cheerful, even though it was the middle of the night.

The dear little lark! It had not flown away after all. And it was truly the most extraordinary bird, for, unlike ordinary larks, it kept hovering about the tower in the silence and darkness of the night, outside the window or over the roof. Whenever he listened for a moment, he heard it singing still.

He went to sleep as happy as a king.

CHAPTER SEVEN

"Happy as a king." How far kings are happy, I cannot say, no more than could Prince Dolor, though he had once been a king himself. But he remembered nothing about it, and there was nobody to tell him, except his nurse, who had been forbidden upon pain of death to let him know anything about his dead parents, or the King his uncle, or, indeed any part of his own history.

Sometimes he speculated about himself, whether he had had a father and mother as other little boys had, what they had been like, and why he had never seen them. But, knowing nothing about them, he did not miss them—only once or twice, reading pretty stories about little children and their mothers, who helped them when they were in difficulty, and comforted them when they were sick, he, feeling ill and dull and lonely, wondered what had become of his mother, and why she never came to see him.

Then, in his history lessons, of course, he read about kings and princes, and the governments of different countries, and the events that happened there. And though he but faintly took in all this, still he did take it in, a little, and worried his young brain about it, and perplexed his nurse with questions, to which she returned sharp and mysterious answers, which only set him thinking the more.

He had plenty of time for thinking. After his last journey in the travelling-cloak, the journey which had given him so much pain, his desire to see the world had somehow faded away. He contented himself with reading his books, and looking out of the tower windows, and listening to his beloved little lark, which had come home with him that day, and never left him again.

True, it kept out of the way; and though his nurse sometimes dimly heard it, and said, "What is that horrid noise outside?" she never got the faintest chance of making it into a lark pie. Prince Dolor had his pet all to himself, and though he seldom saw it, he knew it was near him, and he caught continually, at odd hours of the day, and even in the night, fragments of its delicious song.

All during the winter—so far as there ever was any difference between summer and winter in Hopeless Tower—the little bird cheered and amused him. He scarcely needed anything more —not even his travelling-cloak, which lay bundled up unnoticed in a corner, tied up in its innumerable knots. Nor did his godmother come near him. It seemed as if she had given these treasures and left him alone—to use them, or lose them, apply them, or misapply them, according to his own choice. That is all we can do with children, when they grow into big children, old enough to distinguish between right and wrong, and too old to be forced to do either.

Prince Dolor was now quite a big boy. Not tall—alas! He never could be that, with his poor little shrunken legs; which were of no use, only an encumbrance. But he was stout and strong, with great sturdy shoulders, and muscular arms, upon which he could swing himself about almost like a monkey. As if in compensation for his useless lower limbs, nature had given to these extra strength and activity. His face, too, was very handsome; thinner, firmer, more manly; but still the sweet face of his childhood—his mother's own face.

How his mother would have liked to look at him! Perhaps she did—who knows!

The boy was not a stupid boy either. He could learn almost anything he chose—and he did choose, which was more than half the battle. He never gave up his lessons till he had learnt them all—never thought it a punishment that he had to work at them, and that they cost him a deal of trouble sometimes.

"But," thought he, "men work, and it must be so grand to be a man—a prince too; and I fancy princes work harder than anybody—except kings. The princes I read about generally turn into kings. I wonder"—the boy was always wondering—"Nurse" —and one day he startled her with a sudden question—"tell me—shall I ever be a king?"

The woman stood, perplexed beyond expression. So long a time had passed by since her crime—if it was a crime—and her sentence, that she now seldom thought of either. Even her punishment—to be shut up for life in Hopeless Tower—she had gradually got used to. Used also to the little lame Prince, her charge—whom at first she had hated, though she carefully did everything to keep him alive, since upon him her own life hung. But latterly she had ceased to hate him, and, in a sort of way, almost loved him—at least, enough to be sorry for him—an innocent child, imprisoned here till he grew into an old man— and became a dull, worn-out creature like herself. Sometimes, watching him, she felt more sorry for him than even for herself; and then, seeing she looked a less miserable and ugly woman, he did not shrink from her as usual.

He did not now. "Nurse—dear nurse," said he, "I don't mean to vex you, but tell me—what is a king? Shall I ever be one?"

When she began to think less of herself and more of the child, the woman's courage increased. The idea came to her—what harm would it be, even if he did know his own history? Perhaps he ought to know it—for there had been various ups and downs, usurpations, revolutions, and restorations in Nomansland, as in most other countries. Something might happen —who could tell? Changes might occur. Possibly a crown would even yet be set upon those pretty, fair curls—which she began to think prettier than ever when she saw the imaginary coronet upon them.

She sat down, considering whether her oath, never to "say a word" to Prince Dolor about himself, would be broken, if she were to take a pencil and write what was to be told. A mere quibble—a mean, miserable quibble. But then she was a miserable woman, more to be pitied than scorned.

After long doubt, and with great trepidation, she put her finger to her lips, and taking the Prince's slate—with the sponge tied to it, ready to rub out the writing in a minute—she wrote—

"You are a king."

Prince Dolor started. His face grew pale, and then flushed all over; his eyes glistened; he held himself erect. Lame as he was, anybody could see he was born to be a king.

"Hush!" said his nurse, as he was beginning to speak. And then, terribly frightened all the while—people who have done wrong always are frightened—she wrote down in a few hurried sentences his history. How his parents had died—his uncle had usurped his throne, and sent him to end his days in this lonely tower.

"I, too," added she, bursting into tears. "Unless, indeed, you could get out into the world, and fight for your rights like a man.

And fight for me also, my Prince, that I may not die in this desolate place."

"Poor old nurse!" said the boy compassionately. For somehow, boy as he was, when he heard he was born to be a king, he felt like a man—like a king—who could afford to be tender because he was strong.

He scarcely slept that night, and even though he heard his little lark singing in the sunrise, he barely listened to it. Things more serious and important had taken possession of his mind.

"Suppose," thought he, "I were to do as she says, and go out into the world, no matter how it hurts me—the world of people, active people, as active as that boy I saw. They might only laugh at me—poor helpless creature that I am; but still I might show them I could do something. At any rate, I might go and see if there was anything for me to do. Godmother, help me!"

It was so long since he had asked her help, that he was hardly surprised when he got no answer—only the little lark outside the window sang louder and louder, and the sun rose, flooding the room with light.

Prince Dolor sprang out of bed, and began dressing himself, which was hard work, for he was not used to it—he had always been accustomed to depend upon his nurse for everything.

"But I must now learn to be independent," thought he. "Fancy a king being dressed like a baby!"

So he did the best he could—awkwardly but cheerily—and then he leaped to the corner where lay his travelling-cloak, untied it as before, and watched it unrolling itself—which it did rapidly, with a hearty good-will, as if quite tired of idleness. So was Prince Dolor—or felt as if he was. He jumped into the middle of it, said his charm, and was out through the skylight immediately.

"Good-bye, pretty lark!" he shouted, as he passed it on the wing, still warbling its carol to the newly-risen sun. "You have been my pleasure, my delight; now I must go and work. Sing to old nurse till I come back again. Perhaps she'll hear you— perhaps she won't—but it will do her good all the same. Good-bye!"

But, as the cloak hung irresolute in air, he suddenly remembered that he had not determined where to go—indeed, he did not know, and there was nobody to tell him.

"Godmother," he cried, in much perplexity, "you know what I want—at least, I hope you do, for I hardly do myself—take me where I ought to go; show me whatever I ought to see— never mind what I like to see," as a sudden idea came into his mind that he might see many painful and disagreeable things. But this journey was not for pleasure—as before. He was not a baby now, to do nothing but play—big boys do not always play. Nor men neither—they work. Thus much Prince Dolor knew —though very little more. And as the cloak started off, travelling faster than he had ever known it to do—through sky-land and cloud-land, over freezing mountain-tops, and desolate stretches of forest, and smiling cultivated plains, and great lakes that seemed to him almost as shoreless as the sea—he was often rather frightened. But he crouched down, silent and quiet; what was the use of making a fuss? and, wrapping himself up in his bearskin, waited for what was to happen.

After some time he heard a murmur in the distance, increasing more and more till it grew like the hum of a gigantic hive of bees. And, stretching his chin over the rim of his cloak, Prince Dolor saw—far, far below him, yet with his gold spectacles and silver ears on, he could distinctly hear and see—What?

Most of us have sometime or other visited a great metropolis —have wandered through its network of streets—lost ourselves in its crowds of people—looked up at its tall rows of houses, its grand public buildings, churches, and squares. Also, perhaps, we have peeped into its miserable little back alleys, where dirty children play in gutters all day and half the night—or where men reel tipsy and women fight—where even young boys go about picking pockets, with nobody to tell them it is wrong, except the policeman; and he simply takes them off to prison. And all this wretchedness is close behind the grandeur—like the two sides of the leaf of a book.

An awful sight is a large city, seen anyhow, from anywhere. But, suppose you were to see it from the upper air; where, with your eyes and ears open, you could take in everything at once? What would it look like? How would you feel about it? I hardly know myself. Do you?

Prince Dolor had need to be a king—that is, a boy with a kingly nature—to be able to stand such a sight without being utterly overcome. But he was very much bewildered—as bewildered as a blind person who is suddenly made to see.

He gazed down on the city below him, and then put his hand over his eyes.

"I can't bear to look at it, it is so beautiful—so dreadful. And I don't understand it—not one bit. There is nobody to tell me about it. I wish I had somebody to speak to."

"Do you? Then pray speak to me. I was always considered good at conversation."

The voice that squeaked out this reply was an excellent imitation of the human one, though it came only from a bird. No lark this time, however, but a great black and white creature that flew into the cloak, and began walking round and round on the edge of it with a dignified stride, one foot before the other, like any unfeathered biped you could name.

"I haven't the honour of your acquaintance, sir," said the boy politely.

"Ma'am, if you please. I am a mother bird, and my name is Mag, and I shall be happy to tell you everything you want to know. For I know a great deal; and I enjoy talking. My family is of great antiquity; we have built in this palace for hundreds —that is to say, dozens of years. I am intimately acquainted with the King, the Queen, and the little princes and princesses —also the maids of honour, and all the inhabitants of the city. I talk a good deal, but I always talk sense, and I dare say I should be exceedingly useful to a poor little ignorant boy like you."

"I am a Prince," said the other gently.

"All right. And I am a magpie. You will find me a most respectable bird."

"I have no doubt of it," was the polite answer—though he thought in his own mind that Mag must have a very good opinion of herself. But she was a lady and a stranger, so, of course, he was civil to her.

She settled herself at his elbow, and began to chatter away, pointing out with one skinny claw while she balanced herself on the other, every object of interest—evidently believing, as no doubt all its inhabitants did, that there was no capital in the world like the great metropolis of Nomansland.

I have not seen it, and therefore cannot describe it, so we will just take it upon trust, and suppose it to be, like every other fine city, the finest city that ever was built. "Mag" said so—and of course she knew.

Nevertheless, there were a few things in it which surprised Prince Dolor—and, as he had said, he could not understand them at all. One half the people seemed so happy and busy—hurrying up and down the full streets, or driving lazily along the parks in their grand carriages, while the other half were so wretched and miserable.

"Can't the world be made a little more level? I would try to do it if I were the king."

"But you're not the king: only a little goose of a boy," returned the magpie loftily. "And I'm here not to explain things, only to show them. Shall I show you the royal palace?"

It was a very magnificent palace. It had terraces and gardens, battlements and towers. It extended over acres of ground, and had in it rooms enough to accommodate half the city. Its windows looked in all directions, but none of them had any particular view—except a small one, high up towards the roof, which looked on to the Beautiful Mountains. But since the Queen died there, it had been closed, boarded up, indeed, the magpie said. It was so little and inconvenient, that nobody cared to live in it. Besides, the lower apartments, which had no view, were magnificent—worthy of being inhabited by his Majesty the King.

"I should like to see the King," said Prince Dolor.

But what followed was so important that I must take another chapter to tell it in.

CHAPTER EIGHT

What, I wonder, would be most people's idea of a king? What was Prince Dolor's?

Perhaps a very splendid personage, with a crown on his head, and a sceptre in his hand, sitting on a throne, and judging the people. Always doing right, and never wrong—"The king can do no wrong" was a law laid down in olden times. Never cross, or tired, or sick, or suffering; perfectly handsome and well-dressed, calm and good-tempered, ready to see and hear everybody, and discourteous to nobody; all things always going well with him, and nothing unpleasant ever happening.

This, probably, was what Prince Dolor expected to see. And what did he see? But I must tell you how he saw it.

"Ah," said the magpie, "no levée to-day. The King is ill, though his Majesty does not wish it to be generally known—it would be so very inconvenient. He can't see you, but perhaps you might like to go and take a look at him, in a way I often do? It is so very amusing."

Amusing, indeed!

The Prince was just now too much excited to talk much. Was he not going to see the King, his uncle, who had succeeded his father, and dethroned himself; who had stepped into all the pleasant things that he, Prince Dolor, ought to have had, and shut him up in a desolate tower? What was he like, this great, bad, clever man? Had he got all the things he wanted, which another ought to have had? And did he enjoy them?

"Nobody knows," answered the magpie, just as if she had been sitting inside the Prince's heart, instead of on the top of his shoulder. "He is a king, and that's enough. For the rest nobody knows."

As she spoke Mag flew down on to the palace roof, where the cloak had rested, settling down between the great stacks of chimneys as comfortably as if on the ground. She pecked at the tiles with her beak—truly she was a wonderful bird— and immediately a little hole opened, a sort of door, through which could be seen distinctly the chamber below.

"Now look in, my Prince. Make haste, for I must soon shut it up again."

But the boy hesitated. "Isn't it rude?—won't they think us— intruding?"

"O dear no! There's a hole like this in every palace; dozens of holes, indeed. Everybody knows it, but nobody speaks of it. Intrusion! Why, though the Royal family are supposed to live shut up behind stone walls ever so thick, all the world knows that they live in a glass house where everybody can see them, and throw a stone at them. Now, pop down on your knees, and take a peep at his Majesty."

His Majesty!

The Prince gazed eagerly down, into a large room, the largest room he had ever beheld, with furniture and hangings grander than anything he could have ever imagined. A stray sunbeam, coming through a crevice of the darkened windows, struck across the carpet, and it was the loveliest carpet ever woven— just like a bed of flowers to walk over; only nobody walked over it; the room being perfectly empty and silent.

"Where is the King?" asked the puzzled boy.

"There," said Mag, pointing with one wrinkled claw to a

magnificent bed, large enough to contain six people. In the centre of it, just visible under the silken counterpane—quite straight and still—with its head on the lace pillow—lay a small figure, something like waxwork, fast asleep—very fast asleep! There were a quantity of sparkling rings on the tiny yellow hands, that were curled a little, helplessly, like a baby's, outside the coverlet; the eyes were shut, the nose looked sharp and thin, and the long grey beard hid the mouth, and lay over the breast. A sight not ugly, nor frightening, only solemn and quiet. And so very silent—two little flies buzzing about the curtains of the bed, being the only audible sound.

"Is that the King?" whispered Prince Dolor.

"Yes," replied the bird.

He had been angry—furiously angry; ever since he knew how his uncle had taken the crown, and sent him, a poor little help-less child, to be shut up for life, just as if he had been dead. Many times the boy had felt as if, king as he was, he should like to strike him, this great, strong, wicked man.

Why, you might as well have struck a baby! How helpless he lay, with his eyes shut, and his idle hands folded: they had no more work to do, bad or good.

"What is the matter with him?" asked the Prince again.

"He is dead," said the Magpie with a croak.

No, there was not the least use in being angry with him now. On the contrary, the Prince felt almost sorry for him, except that he looked so peaceful, with all his cares at rest. And this was being dead? So, even kings died?

"Well, well, he hadn't an easy life, folk say, for all his gran-deur. Perhaps he is glad it is over. Good-bye, your Majesty."

With another cheerful tap of her beak, Mistress Mag shut

down the little door in the tiles, and Prince Dolor's first and last sight of his uncle was ended.

He sat in the centre of his travelling-cloak silent and thoughtful.

"What shall we do now?" said the Magpie. "There's nothing much more to be done with his Majesty, except a fine funeral, which I shall certainly go and see. All the world will. He interested the world exceedingly when he was alive, and he ought to do it now he's dead—just once more. And since he can't hear me, I may as well say that, on the whole, his Majesty is much better dead than alive—if we can only get somebody in his place. There'll be such a row in the city presently. Suppose we float up again, and see it all. At a safe distance, though. It will be such fun."

"What will be fun?"

"A revolution."

Whether anybody except a magpie would have called it "fun," I don't know, but it certainly was a remarkable scene.

As soon as the Cathedral bell began to toll, and the minute guns to fire, announcing to the kingdom that it was without a king, the people gathered in crowds, stopping at street corners to talk together. The murmur now and then rose into a shout, and the shout into a roar. When Prince Dolor, quietly floating in upper air, caught the sound of their different and opposite cries, it seemed to him as if the whole city had gone mad together.

"Long live the King!" "The King is dead—down with the King!" "Down with the crown, and the King too!" "Hurrah for the Republic!" "Hurrah for no Government at all."

Such were the shouts which travelled up to the travelling-cloak. And then began—oh, what a scene!

When you children are grown men and women—or before—you will hear and read in books about what are called revolutions—earnestly I trust that neither I nor you may ever see one. But they have happened, and may happen again, in other countries beside Nomansland, when wicked kings have helped to make their people wicked too, or out of an unrighteous nation have sprung rulers equally bad; or, without either of these causes, when a restless country has fancied any change better than no change at all.

For me, I don't like changes, unless pretty sure that they are for good. And how good can come out of absolute evil—the horrible evil that went on this night under Prince Dolor's very eyes—soldiers shooting people down by hundreds in the streets, scaffolds erected, and heads dropping off—houses burnt, and women and children murdered—this is more than I can understand.

But all these things you will find in history, my children, and must by-and-by judge for yourselves the right and wrong of them, as far as anybody ever can judge.

Prince Dolor saw it all. Things happened so fast after one another that they quite confused his faculties.

"Oh, let me go home," he cried at last, stopping his ears and shutting his eyes; "only let me go home!" for even his lonely tower seemed home, and its dreariness and silence absolute paradise after all this.

"Good-bye, then," said the magpie, flapping her wings. She had been chatting incessantly all day and all night, for it was actually thus long that Prince Dolor had been hovering over the city, neither eating nor sleeping, with all these terrible things happening under his very eyes. "You've had enough, I suppose, of seeing the world?"

"Oh, I have—I have!" cried the Prince with a shudder.

"That is, till next time. All right, your Royal Highness. You don't know me, but I know you. We may meet again sometime."

She looked at him with her clear piercing eyes, sharp enough to see through everything, and it seemed as if they changed from bird's eyes to human eyes, the very eyes of his godmother, whom he had not seen for ever so long. But the minute afterwards she became only a bird, and with a screech and a chatter spread her wings and flew away.

Prince Dolor fell into a kind of swoon, of utter misery, bewilderment, and exhaustion, and when he awoke he found himself in his own room—alone and quiet—with the dawn just breaking, and the long rim of yellow light in the horizon glimmering through the window panes.

CHAPTER NINE

When Prince Dolor sat up in bed, trying to remember where he was, whither he had been, and what he had seen the day before, he perceived that his room was empty.

Generally, his nurse rather worried him by breaking his slumbers, coming in and "setting things to rights," as she called it. Now, the dust lay thick upon chairs and tables; there was no harsh voice heard to scold him for not getting up immediately—which, I am sorry to say, this boy did not always do. For he so enjoyed lying still, and thinking lazily, about everything or nothing, that, if he had not tried hard against it, he would certainly have become like those celebrated,

> "Two little men
> Who lay in their bed till the clock struck ten."

It was striking ten now, and still no nurse was to be seen. He was rather relieved at first, for he felt so tired; and besides, when he stretched out his arm, he found to his dismay that he had gone to bed in his clothes.

Very uncomfortable he felt, of course; and just a little frightened. Especially when he began to call and call again, but nobody answered. Often he used to think how nice it would be to get rid of his nurse and live in this tower all by himself—like a sort of monarch, able to do everything he liked, and leave undone all that he did not want to do; but now that this seemed really to have happened, he did not like it at all.

"Nurse—dear nurse—please come back!" he called out. "Come back, and I will be the best boy in all the land."

And when she did not come back, and nothing but silence answered his lamentable call, he very nearly began to cry.

"This won't do," he said at last, dashing the tears from his eyes. "It's just like a baby, and I'm a big boy—shall be a man some day. What has happened, I wonder? I'll go and see."

He sprang out of bed—not to his feet, alas! but to his poor little weak knees, and crawled on them from room to room. All the four chambers were deserted—not forlorn or untidy, for everything seemed to have been done for his comfort—the breakfast and dinner-things were laid, the food spread in order. He might live "like a prince," as the proverb is, for several days. But the place was entirely forsaken—there was evidently not a creature but himself in the solitary tower.

A great fear came upon the poor boy. Lonely as his life had been, he had never known what it was to be absolutely alone. A kind of despair seized him—no violent anger or terror, but a sort of patient desolation.

"What in the world am I to do?" thought he, and sat down in the middle of the floor, half inclined to believe that it would be better to give up entirely, lay himself down and die.

This feeling, however, did not last long, for he was young and strong, and I said before, by nature a very courageous boy. There came into his head, somehow or other, a proverb that his nurse had taught him—the people of Nomansland were very fond of proverbs:

> "For every evil under the sun
>   There is a remedy, or there's none;
>   If there is one, try to find it—
>   If there isn't, never mind it."

"I wonder—is there a remedy now, and could I find it?" cried the Prince, jumping up and looking out of the window.

No help there. He only saw the broad bleak sunshiny plain —that is, at first. But, by-and-by, in the circle of mud that surrounded the base of the tower he perceived distinctly the marks of a horse's feet, and just in the spot where the deaf-mute was accustomed to tie up his great black charger, while he himself ascended, there lay the remains of a bundle of hay and a feed of corn.

"Yes, that's it. He has come and gone, taking nurse away with him. Poor nurse! How glad she would be to go!"

That was Prince Dolor's first thought. His second—wasn't it natural?—was a passionate indignation at her cruelty—at the cruelty of all the world towards him—a poor little helpless boy. Then he determined—forsaken as he was—to try and hold on to the last, and not to die as long as he could possibly help it.

Anyhow, it would be easier to die here than out in the world, among the terrible doings which he had just beheld. From the midst of which, it suddenly struck him, the deaf-mute had come —contrived somehow to make the nurse understand that the King was dead, and she need have no fear in going back to the capital, where there was a grand revolution, and everything turned upside down. So, of course she had gone.

"I hope she'll enjoy it, miserable woman—if they don't cut off her head too."

And then a kind of remorse smote him for feeling so bitterly towards her, after all the years she had taken care of him— grudgingly, perhaps, and coldly; still, she had taken care of him, and that even to the last: for, as I have said, all his four rooms were as tidy as possible, and his meals laid out, that he might have no more trouble than could be helped.

"Possibly she did not mean to be cruel. I won't judge her," said he. And afterwards he was very glad that he had so determined.

For the second time he tried to dress himself, and then to do everything he could for himself—even to sweeping up the hearth and putting on more coals. "It's a funny thing for a prince to have to do," said he laughing. "But my godmother once said princes need never mind doing anything."

And then he thought a little of his godmother. Not of summoning her, or asking her to help him—she had evidently left him to help himself, and he was determined to try his best to do it, being a very proud and independent boy—but he remembered her, tenderly and regretfully, as if even she had been a little hard upon him—poor, forlorn boy that he was! But he seemed to have seen and learned so much within the last few days, that he scarcely felt like a boy, but a man—until he went to bed at night.

When I was a child, I used often to think how nice it would be to live in a little house all by my own self—a house built high up in a tree, or far away in a forest, or halfway up a hillside—so deliciously alone and independent. Not a lesson to learn—but no! I always liked learning my lessons. Anyhow, to choose the lessons I liked best, to have as many books to read and dolls to play with as ever I wanted: above all, to be free and at rest, with nobody to tease, or trouble, or scold me, would be charming. For I was a lonely little thing, who liked quietness—as many children do; which other children, and sometimes grown-up people even, cannot always understand. And so I can understand Prince Dolor.

After his first despair, he was not merely comfortable, but

actually happy in his solitude, doing everything for himself, and enjoying everything by himself—until bedtime.

Then, he did not like it at all. No more, I suppose, than other children would have liked my imaginary house in a tree, when they had had sufficient of their own company.

But the Prince had to bear it—and he did bear it—like a prince: for fully five days. All that time he got up in the morning and went to bed at night, without having spoken to a creature, or, indeed, heard a single sound. For even his little lark was silent: and as for his travelling-cloak, either he never thought about it, or else it had been spirited away—for he made no use of it, nor attempted to do so.

A very strange existence it was, those five lonely days. He never entirely forgot it. It threw him back upon himself, and into himself—in a way that all of us have to learn when we grow up, and are the better for it—but it is somewhat hard learning.

On the sixth day, Prince Dolor had a strange composure in his look, but he was very grave, and thin, and white. He had nearly come to the end of his provisions—and what was to happen next? Get out of the tower he could not; the ladder the deaf mute used was always carried away again; and if it had not been, how could the poor boy have used it? And even if he slung or flung himself down, and by miraculous chance came alive to the foot of the tower, how could he run away?

Fate had been very hard to him, or so it seemed.

He made up his mind to die. Not that he wished to die; on the contrary, there was a great deal that he wished to live to do; but if he must die, he must. Dying did not seem so very dreadful; not even to lie quiet like his uncle, whom he had entirely forgiven now, and neither be miserable nor naughty any more, and escape all those horrible things that he had seen going on outside the palace, in that awful place which was called "the world."

"It's a great deal nicer here," said the poor little Prince, and collected all his pretty things round him: his favourite pictures, which he thought he should like to have near him when he died; his books and toys—no, he had ceased to care for toys now; he only liked them because he had done so as a child. And there he sat very calm and patient, like a king in his castle, waiting for the end.

"Still, I wish I had done something first—something worth doing, that somebody might remember me by," thought he. "Suppose I had grown a man, and had had work to do, and people to care for, and was so useful and busy that they liked me, and perhaps even forgot I was lame. Then, it would have been nice to live, I think."

A tear came into the little fellow's eyes, and he listened intently through the dead silence for some hopeful sound.

Was there one—was it his little lark, whom he had almost forgotten? No, nothing half so sweet. But it really was something—something which came nearer and nearer, so that there was no mistaking it. It was the sound of a trumpet, one of the great silver trumpets so admired in Nomansland. Not pleasant music, but very bold, grand, and inspiring.

As he listened to it the boy seemed to recall many things which had slipped his memory for years, and to nerve himself for whatever might be going to happen.

What had happened was this.

The poor condemned woman had not been such a wicked woman after all. Perhaps her courage was not wholly disinterested, but she had done a very heroic thing. As soon as she heard of the death and burial of the King, and of the changes that were taking place in the country, a daring idea came into her head—to set upon the throne of Nomansland its rightful heir. Thereupon she persuaded the deaf-mute to take her away with him, and they galloped like the wind from city to city, spreading everywhere the news that Prince Dolor's death and burial had been an invention concocted by his wicked uncle— that he was alive and well, and the noblest young Prince that ever was born.

It was a bold stroke, but it succeeded. The country, weary, perhaps, of the late King's harsh rule, and yet glad to save itself from the horrors of the last few days, and the still further horrors of no rule at all, and having no particular interest in the other young princes, jumped at the idea of this Prince, who was the son of their late good King and the beloved Queen Dolorez.

"Hurrah for Prince Dolor! Let Prince Dolor be our sovereign!" rang from end to end of the kingdom. Everybody tried to remember what a dear baby he once was—how like his mother, who had been so sweet and kind, and his father, the finest looking king that ever reigned. Nobody remembered his lameness—or, if they did, they passed it over as a matter of no consequence. They were determined to have him to reign over them, boy as he was—perhaps just because he was a boy, since in that case the great nobles thought they should be able to do as they liked with the country.

Accordingly, with a fickleness not confined to the people of Nomansland, no sooner was the late King laid in his grave than they pronounced him to have been a usurper; turned all his family out of the palace, and left it empty for the reception of the new sovereign, whom they went to fetch with great rejoicing; a select body of lords, gentlemen, and soldiers, travelling night and day in solemn procession through the country, until they reached Hopeless Tower.

There they found the Prince, sitting calmly on the floor—deadly pale indeed, for he expected a quite different end from this, and was resolved if he had to die, to die courageously, like a prince and a king.

But when they hailed him as Prince and King, and explained to him how matters stood, and went down on their knees before him, offering the crown (on a velvet cushion, with four golden tassels, each nearly as big as his head)—small though he was and lame, which lameness the courtiers pretended not to notice—there came such a glow into his face, such a dignity into his demeanour, that he became beautiful, king-like.

"Yes," he said, "if you desire it, I will be your king. And I will do my best to make my people happy."

Then there arose, from inside and outside the tower, such a shout as never yet was heard across the lonely plain.

Prince Dolor shrank a little from the deafening sound. "How shall I be able to rule all this great people? You forget, my lords, that I am only a little boy still."

"Not so very little," was the respectful answer. "We have searched in the records, and found that your Royal Highness—your Majesty, I mean—is precisely fifteen years old."

"Am I?" said Prince Dolor; and his first thought was a thoroughly childish pleasure that he should now have a birthday, with a whole nation to keep it. Then he remembered that his childish days were done. He was a monarch now. Even his nurse, to whom, the moment he saw her, he had held out his hand, kissed it reverently, and called him ceremoniously "his Majesty the King."

"A king must be always a king, I suppose," said he half sadly, when, the ceremonies over, he had been left to himself for just ten minutes, to put off his boy's clothes and be re-attired in magnificent robes, before he was conveyed away from his tower to the Royal Palace.

He could take nothing with him; indeed, he soon saw that, however politely they spoke, they would not allow him to take anything. If he was to be their king, he must give up his old life for ever. So he looked with tender farewell on his old books, old toys, the furniture he knew so well, and the familiar plain in all its levelness, ugly yet pleasant, simply because it was familiar.

"It will be a new life in a new world," said he to himself: "but I'll remember the old things still. And, oh! if before I go, I could but once see my dear old godmother."

While he spoke, he had laid himself down on the bed for a minute or two, rather tired with his grandeur, and confused by the noise of the trumpets which kept playing incessantly down below. He gazed, half sadly, up to the skylight, whence there came pouring a stream of sun-rays, with innumerable motes floating there, like a bridge thrown between heaven and earth. Sliding down it, as if she had been made of air, came the little old woman in grey.

So beautiful looked she—old as she was—that Prince Dolor was at first quite startled by the apparition. Then he held out his arms in eager delight.

"O, godmother, you have not forsaken me!"

"Not at all, my son. You may not have seen me, but I have seen you, many a time."

"How?"

"O, never mind. I can turn into anything I please, you know.

And I have been a bearskin rug, and a crystal goblet—and sometimes I have changed from inanimate to animate nature, put on feathers, and made myself very comfortable as a bird."

"Ha!" laughed the Prince, a new light breaking in upon him, as he caught the infection of her tone, lively and mischievous. "Ha, ha! a lark, for instance?"

"Or a magpie," answered she, with a capital imitation of Mistress Mag's croaky voice. "Do you suppose I am always sentimental and never funny?—If anything makes you happy, gay or grave, don't you think it is more than likely to come through your old godmother?"

"I believe that," said the boy tenderly, holding out his arms. They clasped one another in a close embrace.

Suddenly Prince Dolor looked very anxious. "You will not leave me now that I am a king? Otherwise, I had rather not be a king at all. Promise never to forsake me?"

The little old woman laughed gaily. "Forsake you? That is impossible. But it is just possible you may forsake me. Not probable though. Your mother never did, and she was a queen. The sweetest queen in all the world was the lady Dolorez."

"Tell me about her," said the boy eagerly. "As I get older I think I can understand more. Do tell me."

"Not now. You couldn't hear me for the trumpets and the shouting. But when you are come to the palace, ask for a long-closed upper room, which looks out upon the Beautiful Mountains; open it and take it for your own. Whenever you go there, you will always find me, and we will talk together about all sorts of things."

"And about my mother?"

The little old woman nodded—and kept nodding and smiling to herself many times, as the boy repeated over and over again the sweet words he had never known or understood—"my mother—my mother."

"Now I must go," said she, as the trumpets blared louder and louder, and the shouts of the people showed that they would not endure any delay. "Good-bye, Good-bye! Open the window and out I fly."

Prince Dolor repeated gaily the musical rhyme—but all the while tried to hold his godmother fast.

Vain, vain—for the moment that a knocking was heard at his door, the sun went behind a cloud, the bright stream of dancing motes vanished, and the little old woman with them —he knew not where.

So Prince Dolor quitted his tower—which he had entered so mournfully and ignominiously, as a little helpless baby carried in the deaf-mute's arms—quitted it as the great King of No-mansland.

The only thing he took away with him was something so insignificant, that none of the lords, gentlemen, and soldiers who escorted him with such triumphant splendour, could possibly notice it—a tiny bundle, which he had found lying on the floor just where the bridge of sunbeams had rested. At once he had pounced upon it, and thrust it secretly into his bosom, where it dwindled into such small proportions, that it might have been taken for a mere chest-comforter—a bit of flannel— or an old pocket-handkerchief!

It was his travelling-cloak.

CHAPTER TEN

Did Prince Dolor become a great king? Was he, though little more than a boy, "the father of his people," as all kings ought to be? Did his reign last long—long and happy?—and what were the principal events of it, as chronicled in the history of Nomansland?

Why, if I were to answer all these questions, I should have to write another book. And I'm tired, children, tired—as grown-up people sometimes are; though not always with play. (Besides, I have a small person belonging to me, who, though she likes extremely to listen to the word-of-mouth story of this book, grumbles much at the writing of it, and has run about the house clapping her hands with joy when mamma told her that it was nearly finished. But that is neither here nor there.)

I have related, as well as I could, the history of Prince Dolor, but with the history of Nomansland I am as yet unacquainted. If anybody knows it, perhaps he or she will kindly write it all down in another book. But mine is done.

However, of this I am sure, that Prince Dolor made an excellent king. Nobody ever does anything less well, not even the commonest duty of common daily life, for having such a godmother as the little old woman clothed in grey, whose name is—well, I leave you to guess. Nor, I think, is anybody less good, less capable of both work and enjoyment in after life, for having been a little unhappy in his youth, as the Prince had been.

I cannot take upon myself to say that he was always happy

now—who is?—or that he had no cares; just show me the person who is quite free from them! But, whenever people worried and bothered him—as they did sometimes, with state etiquette, state squabbles, and the like, setting up themselves and pulling down their neighbours—he would take refuge in that upper room which looked out on the Beautiful Mountains, and laying his head on his godmother's shoulder, become calmed and at rest.

Also, she helped him out of any difficulty which now and then occurred—for there never was such a wise old woman. When the people of Nomansland raised the alarm—as sometimes they did—for what people can exist without a little fault-finding?—and began to cry out, "Unhappy is the nation whose king is a child," she would say to him gently, "You are a child. Accept the fact. Be humble—be teachable. Lean upon the wisdom of others till you have gained your own."

He did so. He learned how to take advice before attempting to give it, to obey before he could righteously command. He assembled round him all the good and wise of his kingdom—laid all its affairs before them, and was guided by their opinions until he had maturely formed his own.

This he did, sooner than anybody would have imagined, who did not know of his godmother and his travelling-cloak—two secret blessings, which, though many guessed at, nobody quite understood. Nor did they understand why he loved so the little upper room, except that it had been his mother's room, from the window of which, as people remembered now, she had used to sit for hours watching the Beautiful Mountains.

Out of that window he used to fly—not very often; as he grew older, the labours of state prevented the frequent use of his travelling-cloak; still he did use it sometimes. Only now it was less for his own pleasure and amusement than to see something, or investigate something, for the good of the country. But he prized his godmother's gift as dearly as ever. It was a comfort to him in all his vexations; an enhancement of all his joys. It made him almost forget his lameness—which was never cured.

However, the cruel things which had been once foreboded of him did not happen. His misfortune was not such a heavy one after all. It proved to be much less inconvenience, even to himself, than had been feared. A council of eminent surgeons and mechanicians invented for him a wonderful pair of crutches, with the help of which, though he never walked easily or gracefully, he did manage to walk, so as to be quite independent. And such was the love his people bore him, that they never heard the sound of his crutch on the marble palace-floors without a leap of the heart, for they knew that good was coming to them whenever he approached them.

Thus, though he never walked in processions, never reviewed his troops mounted on a magnificent charger, nor did any of the things which make a show monarch so much appreciated, he was able for all the duties and a great many of the pleasures of his rank. When he held his levées, not standing, but seated on a throne, ingeniously contrived to hide his infirmity, the people thronged to greet him; when he drove out through the city streets, shouts followed him wherever he went—every countenance brightened as he passed, and his own, perhaps, was the brightest of all.

First, because, accepting his affliction as inevitable, he took it patiently; second, because, being a brave man, he bore it bravely; trying to forget himself, and live out of himself, and in and for other people. Therefore other people grew to love him so well, that I think hundreds of his subjects might have been found who were almost ready to die for their poor lame King.

He never gave them a queen. When they implored him to choose one, he replied that his country was his bride, and he desired no other. But, perhaps, the real reason was that he shrank from any change; and that no wife in all the world would have been found so perfect, so lovable, so tender to him in all his weaknesses, as his beautiful old godmother.

His four-and-twenty other godfathers and godmothers, or as many of them as were still alive, crowded round him as soon as he ascended the throne. He was very civil to them all, but adopted none of the names they had given him, keeping to the one by which he had been always known, though it had now almost lost its meaning; for King Dolor was one of the happiest and cheerfullest men alive.

He did a good many things, however, unlike most men and most kings, which a little astonished his subjects. First, he pardoned the condemned woman, who had been his nurse, and ordained that from henceforward there should be no such thing as the punishment of death in Nomansland. All capital criminals were to be sent to perpetual imprisonment in Hopeless Tower, and the plain round about it, where they could do no harm to anybody, and might in time do a little good, as the woman had done.

Another surprise he shortly afterwards gave the nation. He recalled his uncle's family, who had fled away in terror to another country, and restored them to all their honours in their own. By-and-by he chose the eldest son of his eldest cousin (who had been dead a year), and had him educated in the royal palace, as the heir to the throne. This little Prince was a quiet, unobtrusive boy, so that everybody wondered at the King's choosing him, when there were so many more; but as he grew into a fine young fellow, good and brave, they agreed that the King judged more wisely than they.

"Not a lame prince neither," his Majesty observed one day, watching him affectionately; for he was the best runner, the highest leaper, the keenest and most active sportsman in the country. "One cannot make oneself, but one can sometimes help a little in the making of somebody else. It is well."

This was said, not to any of his great lords and ladies, but to a good old woman—his first homely nurse—whom he had sought for far and wide, and at last found, in her cottage among the Beautiful Mountains. He sent for her to visit him once a year, and treated her with great honour until she died. He was equally kind, though somewhat less tender, to his other nurse, who, after receiving her pardon, returned to her native town and grew into a great lady, and I hope a good one. But as she was so grand a personage now, any little faults she had did not show.

Thus King Dolor's reign passed, year after year, long and prosperous. Whether he was happy—"as happy as a king"—is a question no human being can decide. But I think he was, because he had the power of making everybody about him happy, and did it too; also because he was his godmother's godson, and could shut himself up with her whenever he liked, in that quiet little room, in view of the Beautiful Mountains, which nobody else ever saw or cared to see. They were too far off, and the city lay so low. But there they were, all the time. No change ever came to them; and I think, at any day throughout his long reign, the King would sooner have lost his crown than have lost sight of the Beautiful Mountains.

In course of time, when the little prince, his cousin, was grown into a tall young man, capable of all the duties of a man, his Majesty did one of the most extraordinary acts ever known

in a sovereign beloved by his people and prosperous in his reign.
He announced that he wished to invest his heir with the royal
purple—at any rate, for a time—while he himself went away on
a distant journey, whither he had long desired to go.

Everybody marvelled, but nobody opposed him. Who could
oppose the good King, who was not a young king now? And,
besides, the nation had a great admiration for the young Regent—and, possibly, a lurking pleasure in change.

So there was fixed a day, when all the people whom it would
hold, assembled in the great square of the capital, to see the
young prince installed solemnly in his new duties, and under-
taking his new vows. He was a very fine young fellow; tall and
straight as a poplar tree, with a frank handsome face—a great
deal handsomer than the King, some people said, but others
thought differently. However, as his Majesty sat on his throne,
with his grey hair falling from underneath his crown, and a
few wrinkles showing in spite of his smile, there was something
about his countenance which made his people, even while they
shouted, regard him with a tenderness mixed with awe.

He lifted up his thin, slender hand, and there came a silence
over the vast crowd immediately. Then he spoke, in his own
accustomed way, using no grand words, but saying what he had
to say in the simplest fashion, though with a clearness that
struck their ears like the first song of a bird in the dusk of the
morning.

"My people, I am tired: I want to rest. I have had a long
reign, and done much work—at least, as much as I was able to
do. Many might have done it better than I—but none with a
better will. Now I leave it to others. I am tired, very tired. Let
me go home."

There rose a murmur—of content or discontent none could

well tell; then it died down again, and the assembly listened silently once more.

"I am not anxious about you—my people—my children," continued the King. "You are prosperous and at peace. I leave you in good hands. The Prince Regent will be a fitter king for you than I."

"No, no, no!" rose the universal shout—and those who had sometimes found fault with him shouted louder than anybody. But he seemed as if he heard them not.

"Yes, yes," said he, as soon as the tumult had a little subsided: and his voice sounded firm and clear; and some very old people, who boasted of having seen him as a child, declared that his face took a sudden change, and grew as young and sweet as that of the little Prince Dolor. "Yes, I must go. It is time for me to go. Remember me sometimes, my people, for I have loved you well. And I am going a long way, and I do not think I shall come back any more."

He drew a little bundle out of his breast pocket—a bundle that nobody had ever seen before. It was small and shabby-looking, and tied up with many knots, which untied themselves in an instant. With a joyful countenance, he muttered over it a few half-intelligible words. Then, so suddenly that even those nearest to his Majesty could not tell how it came about, the King was away—away—floating right up in the air —upon something, they knew not what, except that it appeared to be as safe and pleasant as the wings of a bird.

And after him sprang a bird—a dear little lark, rising from whence no one could say, since larks do not usually build their nests in the pavement of city squares. But there it was, a real lark, singing far over their heads, louder, and clearer, and more joyful, as it vanished further into the blue sky.

Shading their eyes, and straining their ears, the astonished people stood, until the whole vision disappeared like a speck in the clouds—the rosy clouds that overhung the Beautiful Mountains.

Then they guessed that they should see their beloved king no more. Well-beloved as he was, he had always been somewhat of a mystery to them, and such he remained. But they went home, and, accepting their new monarch, obeyed him faithfully for his cousin's sake.

King Dolor was never again beheld or heard of in his own country. But the good he had done there lasted for years and years; he was long missed and deeply mourned—at least, so far as anybody could mourn one who was gone on such a happy journey.

Whither he went, or who went with him, it is impossible to say. But I myself believe that his godmother took him, on his travelling-cloak, to the Beautiful Mountains. What he did there, or where he is now, who can tell? I cannot. But one thing I am quite sure of, that, wherever he is, he is perfectly happy.

And so, when I think of him, am I.

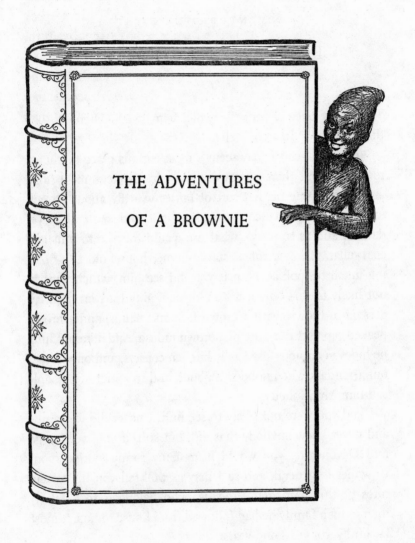

THE ADVENTURES

OF A BROWNIE

BROWNIE AND THE COOK

There was once a little Brownie, who lived—where do you think he lived? In a coal-cellar.

Now a coal-cellar may seem a most curious place to choose to live in: but then a Brownie is a curious creature—a fairy, and yet not one of that sort of fairies who fly about on gossamer wings, and dance in the moonlight, and so on. He never dances: and as to wings, what use would they be to him in a coal-cellar? He is a sober, stay-at-home, household elf—nothing much to look at, even if you did see him, which you are not likely to do—only a little old man, about a foot high, all dressed in brown, with a brown face and hands, and a brown peaked cap, just the color of a brown mouse. And, like a mouse, he hides in corners—especially kitchen corners, and only comes out after dark when nobody is about, and so sometimes people call him Mr. Nobody.

I said you were not likely to see him. I never did, certainly, and never knew anybody that did; but still, if you were to go into Devonshire, you would hear many funny stories about Brownies in general, and so I may as well tell you the adventures of this particular Brownie, who belonged to a family there; which family he had followed from house to house, most faithfully, for years and years.

A good many people had heard him—or supposed they had —when there were extraordinary noises about the house; noises which must have come from a mouse or a rat—or a Brownie.

But nobody had ever seen him except the children—the three little boys and three little girls—who declared he often came to play with them when they were alone and was the nicest companion in the world, though he was such an old man—hundreds of years old! He was full of fun and mischief, and up to all sorts of tricks, but he never did anybody any harm unless they deserved it.

Brownie was supposed to live under one particular coal, in the darkest corner of the cellar, which was never allowed to be disturbed. Why he had chosen it nobody knew, and how he lived there nobody knew either, nor what he lived upon. Except that, ever since the family could remember, there had always been a bowl of milk put behind the coal-cellar door for the Brownie's supper. Perhaps he drank it—perhaps he didn't; anyhow the bowl was always found empty next morning. The old cook, who had lived all her life in the family, had never once forgotten to give Brownie his supper; but at last she died, and a young cook came in her stead, who was very apt to forget everything. She was also both careless and lazy, and disliked taking the trouble to put a bowl of milk in the same place every night for Mr. Nobody. "I don't believe in Brownies," she said; "I have never seen one, and seeing's believing." So she laughed at the other servants, who looked very grave, and put the bowl of milk in its place as often as they could, without saying much about it.

But once, when Brownie woke up at his usual hour for rising—ten o'clock at night, and looked round in search of his supper—which was, in fact, his breakfast—he found nothing there. At first he could not imagine such neglect, and went smelling and smelling about for his bowl of milk—it was not always placed in the same corner now—but in vain.

"This will never do," said he; and, being extremely hungry, began running about the coal-cellar to see what he could find. His eyes were as useful in the dark as in the light—like a pussy-cat's; but there was nothing to be seen—not even a potato paring, or a dry crust, or a well-gnawed bone such as Tiny the terrier sometimes brought into the coal-cellar and left on the floor—nothing, in short, but heaps of coals and coal-dust; and even a Brownie cannot eat that, you know.

"Can't stand this; quite impossible!" said the Brownie, tightening his belt to make his poor little inside feel less empty. He had been asleep so long—about a week, I believe, as was his habit when there was nothing to do—that he seemed ready to eat his own head, or his boots, or anything. "What's to be done? Since nobody brings my supper, I must go and fetch it."

He spoke quickly, for he always thought quickly, and made up his mind in a minute. To be sure, it was a very little mind, like his little body; but he did the best he could with it, and was not a bad sort of old fellow, after all. In the house he had never done any harm, and often some good, for he frightened away all the rats, mice, and black beetles. Not the crickets—he liked them, as the old cook had done: she said they were such cheerful creatures, and always brought luck to the house. But the young cook could not bear them, and used to pour boiling water down their holes, and set basins of beer for them with little wooden bridges up to the rim, that they might walk up, tumble in, and be drowned.

So there was not even a cricket singing in the silent house when Brownie put his head out of his coal-cellar door, which, to his surprise, he found open. Old cook used to lock it every night, but the young cook had left that key, and the kitchen and pantry keys too, all dangling in the lock, so that any thief might have got in and wandered all over the house without being found out.

"Hurrah, here's luck!" cried Brownie, tossing his cap up in the air, and bounding right through the scullery into the kitchen. It was quite empty, but there was a good fire burning itself out—just for its own amusement, and the remains of a capital supper spread on the table—enough for half a dozen people being left still.

Would you like to know what there was? Devonshire cream, of course; and part of a large dish of junket, which is something like curds and whey. Lots of bread-and-butter and cheese, and half an apple-pudding. Also a great jug of cider and another of milk, and several half-full glasses, and no end of dirty plates, knives, and forks. All were scattered about the table in a most untidy fashion, just as the servants had risen from their supper, without thinking to put anything away.

Brownie screwed up his little old face and turned up his button of a nose, and gave a long whistle. You might not believe it, seeing he lived in a coal-cellar; but really he liked tidiness, and always played his pranks upon disorderly or slovenly folk.

"Whew!" said he. "Here's a chance. What a supper I'll get now!"

And he jumped on to a chair and thence to the table, but so quietly that the large black cat with four white paws, called Muff, because she was so fat and soft and her fur so long, who sat dozing in front of the fire, just opened one eye and went to sleep again. She had tried to get her nose into the milk-jug, but it was too small; and the junket-dish was too deep for her to reach, except with one paw. She didn't care much for bread and cheese and apple-pudding, and was very well fed besides; so,

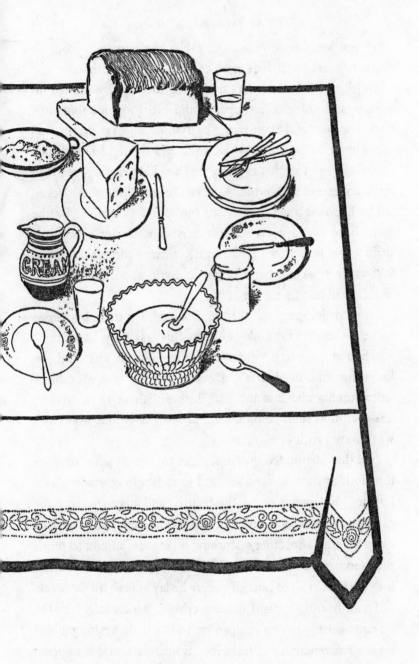

after just wandering round the table, she had jumped down from it again and settled herself to sleep on the hearth.

But Brownie had no notion of going to sleep. He wanted his supper, and oh! what a supper he did eat! First one thing and then another, and then trying everything all over again. And oh! what a lot he drank!—First milk and then cider, and then mixed the two together in a way that would have disagreed with anybody except a Brownie. As it was he was obliged to slacken his belt several times, and at last took it off altogether. But he must have had a most extraordinary capacity for eating and drinking—since, after he had nearly cleared the table, he was just as lively as ever, and began jumping about on the table as if he had had no supper at all.

Now his jumping was a little awkward, for there happened to be a clean white table-cloth: as this was only Monday, it had had no time to get dirty—untidy as the cook was. And you know Brownie lived in a coal-cellar, and his feet were black with running about in the coal dust. So wherever he trod he left the impression behind, until at last the whole table-cloth was covered with black marks.

Not that he minded this; in fact, he took great pains to make the cloth as dirty as possible; and then laughing loudly, "Ho! ho! ho!" he leaped on to the hearth, and began teasing the cat; squeaking like a mouse, or chirping like a cricket, or buzzing like a fly: and altogether disturbing poor pussy's mind so much that she went and hid herself in the furthest corner, and left him the hearth all to himself, where he lay at ease till daybreak.

Then, hearing a slight noise overhead, which might be the servants getting up, he jumped on to the table again, gobbled up the few remaining crumbs for his breakfast, and scampered off to his coal-cellar, where he hid himself under his big coal, and fell asleep for the day.

Well, the cook came downstairs rather earlier than usual, for she remembered she had to clear off the remains of supper; but lo and behold, there was nothing left to clear! Every bit of food was eaten up—the cheese looked as if a dozen mice had been nibbling at it, and nibbled it down to the very rind; the milk and cider were all drunk—and mice don't care for milk and cider, you know. As for the apple-pudding, it had vanished altogether; and the dish was licked as clean as if Boxer, the yard-dog, had been at it in his hungriest mood.

"And my white table-cloth—oh, my clean white table-cloth! What can have been done to it?" cried she, in amazement. For it was all over little black foot-marks, just the size of a baby's foot—only babies don't wear shoes with nails in them, and don't run about and climb on kitchen tables after all the family have gone to bed.

Cook was a little frightened; but her fright changed to anger when she saw the large black cat stretched comfortably on the hearth. Poor Muff had crept there for a little snooze after Brownie went away.

"You nasty cat! I see it all now; it's you that have eaten up all the supper; it's you that have been on my clean table-cloth with your dirty paws."

They were white paws, and as clean as possible; but cook never thought of that, any more than she did of the fact that cats don't usually drink cider or eat apple-pudding.

"I'll teach you to come stealing food in this way; take that —and that—and that!"

Cook got hold of a broom and beat poor pussy till the creature ran mewing away. She couldn't speak, you know—unfortunate cat! and tell people that it was Brownie who had done it all.

Next night cook thought she would make all safe and sure; so, instead of letting the cat sleep by the fire, she shut her up in the chilly coal-cellar, locked the door, put the key in her pocket, and went off to bed—leaving the supper as before.

When Brownie woke up and looked out of his hole, there was, as usual, no supper for him, and the cellar was close shut. He peered about, to try and find some cranny under the door to creep out at, but there was none. And he felt so hungry that he could almost have eaten the cat, who kept walking to and fro in a melancholy manner—only she was alive, and he couldn't well eat her alive; besides, he knew she was old, and had an idea she might be tough; so he merely said politely, "How do you do, Mrs. Pussy?" to which she answered nothing —of course.

Something must be done, and luckily Brownies can do things which nobody else can do. So he thought he would change himself into a mouse, and gnaw a hole through the door. But then he suddenly remembered the cat, who, though he had decided not to eat her, might take this opportunity of eating him. So he thought it advisable to wait till she was fast asleep, which did not happen for a good while. At length, quite tired with walking about, pussy turned round on her tail six times, curled down in a corner, and fell fast asleep.

Immediately Brownie changed himself into the smallest mouse possible; and, taking care not to make the least noise, gnawed a hole in the door and squeezed himself through, immediately turning into his proper shape again, for fear of accidents.

The kitchen fire was at its last glimmer; but it showed a better supper than even last night, for the cook had had friends with her—a brother and two cousins—and they had been exceedingly merry. The food they had left behind was enough for three Brownies at least, but this one managed to eat it all up. Only once, in trying to cut a great slice of beef, he let the carving-knife and fork fall with such a clatter that Tiny the terrier, who was tied up at the foot of the stairs, began to bark furiously. However, he brought her her puppy, which had been left in a basket in a corner of the kitchen, and so succeeded in quieting her.

After that he enjoyed himself amazingly, and made more marks than ever on the white table-cloth; for he began jumping about like a pea on a trencher, in order to make his particularly large supper agree with him.

Then, in the absence of the cat, he teased the puppy for an hour or two, till, hearing the clock strike five, he thought it as well to turn into a mouse again and creep back cautiously into his cellar. He was only just in time, for Muff opened one eye, and was just going to pounce upon him, when he changed himself into a Brownie. She was so startled that she bounded away, her tail growing into twice its natural size, and her eyes gleaming like round green globes. But Brownie only said, "Ha! ha! ho!" and walked deliberately into his hole.

When cook came downstairs and saw that the same thing had happened again—that the supper was all eaten, and the table-cloth blacker than ever with the extraordinary foot-marks, she was greatly puzzled. Who could have done it all? Not the cat, who came mewing out of the coal-cellar the minute she unlocked the door. Possibly a rat—but then would a rat have come within reach of Tiny?

"It must have been Tiny herself, or her puppy," which just

came rolling out of its basket over cook's feet. "You little wretch! You and your mother are the greatest nuisance imaginable. I'll punish you!"

And, quite forgetting that Tiny had been safely tied up all night and that her poor little puppy was so fat and helpless it could scarcely stand on its legs, to say nothing of jumping on chairs and tables, she gave them both such a thrashing that they ran howling together out of the kitchen door, where the kind little kitchen-maid took them up in her arms.

"You ought to have beaten the Brownie, if you could catch him," said she, in a whisper. "He'll do it again and again, you'll see, for he can't bear an untidy kitchen. You'd better do as poor old cook did, and clear the supper things away, and put the odds and ends safe in the larder; also," she added mysteriously, "if I were you, I'd put a bowl of milk behind the coal-cellar door."

"Nonsense!" answered the young cook, and flounced away. But afterward she thought better of it, and did as she was advised, grumbling all the time, but doing it.

Next morning the milk was gone! Perhaps Brownie had drunk it up; anyhow nobody could say that he hadn't. As for the supper, cook having safely laid it on the shelves of the larder, nobody touched it. And the table-cloth, which was wrapped up tidily and put in the dresser drawer, came out as clean as ever, with not a single black foot-mark upon it. No mischief being done, the cat and the dog both escaped beating, and Brownie played no more tricks with anybody—till the next time.

BROWNIE AND THE CHERRY-TREE

The "next time" was quick in coming, which was not wonderful, considering there was a Brownie in the house. Otherwise the house was like most other houses, and the family like most other families. The children also: they were sometimes good, sometimes naughty, like other children; but, on the whole, they deserved to have the pleasure of a Brownie to play with them, as they declared he did—many a time.

A favorite play-place was the orchard, where grew the biggest cherry-tree you ever saw. They called it their "castle," because it rose up ten feet from the ground in one thick stem, and then branched out into a circle of boughs, with a flat place in the middle, where two or three children could sit at once. There they often did sit, turn by turn, or one at a time—sometimes with a book, reading; and the biggest boy made a sort of rope-ladder by which they could climb up and down—which they did all winter, and enjoyed their "castle" very much.

But one day in spring they found their ladder cut away! The gardener had done it, saying it injured the tree, which was just coming into blossom. Now this gardener was a rather gruff man, with a growling voice. He did not mean to be unkind, but he disliked children; he said they bothered him. But when they complained to their mother about the ladder, she agreed with the gardener that the tree must not be injured, as it bore the biggest cherries in all the neighborhood—so big that the old saying of "taking two bites at a cherry" came really true.

"Wait till the cherries are ripe," said she; and so the little people waited, and watched it through its leafing and blossoming—such sheets of blossom, white as snow!—till the fruit began to show, and grew large and red on every bough.

At last one morning the mother said, "Children, should you like to help gather the cherries to-day?"

"Hurrah!" they cried, "and not a day too soon; for we saw a flock of starlings in the next field—and if we don't clear the tree, they will."

"Very well; clear it then. Only mind and fill my basket quite full, for preserving. What is over you may eat, if you like."

"Thank you, thank you!" and the children were eager to be off; but the mother stopped them till she could get the gardener and his ladder.

"For it is he must climb the tree, not you; and you must do exactly as he tells you; and he will stop with you all the time and see that you don't come to harm."

This was no slight cloud on the children's happiness, and they begged hard to go alone.

"Please might we? We will be so good!"

The mother shook her head. All the goodness in the world would not help them if they tumbled off the tree, or ate themselves sick with cherries. "You would not be safe, and I should be so unhappy!"

To make mother "unhappy" was the worst rebuke possible to these children; so they choked down their disappointment and followed the gardener as he walked on ahead, carrying his ladder on his shoulder. He looked very cross, and as if he did not like the children's company at all.

They were pretty good, on the whole, though they chattered a good deal; but the gardener said not a word to them all the way to the orchard. When they reached it, he just told them to "keep out of his way and not worrit him," which they politely promised, saying among themselves that they should not enjoy their cherry-gathering at all. But children who make the best of things and try to be as good as they can sometimes have fun unawares.

When the gardener was steadying his ladder against the trunk of the cherry-tree, there was suddenly heard the barking of a dog, and a very fierce dog, too. First it seemed close beside them, then in the flower-garden, and then in the fowl-yard.

The gardener dropped the ladder out of his hands. "It's that Boxer! He has got loose again! He will be running after my chickens, and dragging his broken chain all over my borders. And he is so fierce, and so delighted to get free. He'll bite anybody who ties him up, except me."

"Hadn't you better go and see after him?"

The gardener thought it was the eldest boy who spoke, and turned round angrily; but the little fellow had never opened his lips.

Here there was heard a still louder bark, and from a quite different part of the garden.

"There he is—I'm sure of it! Jumping over my bedding-out plants, and breaking my cucumber frames. Abominable beast! —just let me catch him!"

Off the gardener darted in a violent passion, throwing the ladder down upon the grass, and forgetting all about the cherries and the children.

The instant he was gone, a shrill laugh, loud and merry, was heard close by, and a little brown old man's face peeped from behind the cherry-tree.

"How d'ye do? Boxer was me. Didn't I bark well? Now I'm come to play with you."

The children clapped their hands; for they knew they were going to have some fun if Brownie was there—he was the best little playfellow in the world. And then they had him all to themselves. Nobody ever saw him except the children.

"Come on!" cried he, in his shrill voice, half like an old man's, half like a baby's. "Who'll begin to gather the cherries?"

They all looked blank; for the tree was so high to where the branches sprung, and besides, their mother had said they were not to climb. And the ladder lay flat upon the grass—far too heavy for little hands to move.

"What! You big boys don't expect a poor little fellow like me to lift the ladder all by myself? Try! I'll help you."

Whether he helped or not, no sooner had they taken hold of the ladder than it rose up, almost of its own accord, and fixed itself quite safely against the tree.

"But we must not climb—mother told us not," said the boys ruefully. "Mother said we were to stand at the bottom and pick up the cherries."

"Very well. Obey your mother. I'll just run up the tree myself."

Before the words were out of his mouth Brownie had darted up the ladder like a monkey, and disappeared among the fruit-laden branches.

The children looked dismayed for a minute till they saw a merry brown face peeping out from the green leaves at the very top of the tree.

"Biggest fruit always grows highest," cried the Brownie. "Stand in a row, all you children. Little boys, hold out your caps: little girls, make a bag of your pinafores. Open your mouths and shut your eyes, and see what the queen will send you."

They laughed and did as they were told; whereupon they were drowned in a shower of cherries—cherries falling like hail-stones, hitting them on their heads, their cheeks, their noses—filling their caps and pinafores, and then rolling and tumbling on to the grass, till it was strewn thick as leaves in autumn with the rosy fruit.

What a glorious scramble they had—these three little boys and three little girls! How they laughed and jumped and knocked heads together in picking up the cherries, yet never quarreled—for there were such heaps, it would have been ridiculous to squabble over them; and besides, whenever they began to quarrel, Brownie always ran away. Now he was the merriest of the lot; ran up and down the tree like a cat, helped to pick up the cherries, and was first-rate at filling the large market-basket.

"We were to eat as many as we liked, only we must first fill the basket," conscientiously said the eldest girl; upon which they all set to at once, and filled it to the brim.

"Now we'll have a dinner-party," cried the Brownie; and squatted down like a Turk, crossing his queer little legs and sticking his elbows upon his knees in a way that nobody but a Brownie could manage. "Sit in a ring! Sit in a ring! and we'll see who can eat fastest."

The children obeyed. How many cherries they devoured, and how fast they did it, passes my capacity of telling. I only hope they were not ill next day, and that all the cherry-stones they swallowed by mistake did not disagree with them. But perhaps nothing does disagree with one when one dines with a Brownie. They ate so much, laughing in equal proportion, that they had

quite forgotten the gardener—when, all of a sudden, they heard him clicking angrily the orchard gate, and talking to himself as he walked through.

"That nasty dog! It wasn't Boxer, after all. A nice joke! to find him quietly asleep in his kennel after having hunted him, as I thought, from one end of the garden to the other! Now for the cherries and the children—bless us, where are the children? And the cherries? Why, the tree is as bare as a blackthorn in February! The starlings have been at it, after all. Oh, dear! oh, dear!"

"Oh, dear! oh, dear!" echoed a voice from behind the tree, followed by shouts of mocking laughter. Not from the children —they sat as demure as possible, all in a ring, with their hands before them, and in the center the huge basket of cherries, piled as full as it could possibly hold. But the Brownie had disappeared.

"You naughty brats, I'll have you punished!" cried the gardener, furious at the laughter, for he never laughed himself. But as there was nothing wrong, the cherries being gathered—a very large crop and the ladder found safe in its place—it was difficult to say what had been the harm done and who had done it.

So he went growling back to the house, carrying the cherries to the mistress, who coaxed him into good temper again, as she sometimes did; bidding also the children to behave well to him, since he was an old man, and not really bad—only cross. As for the little folks, she had not the slightest intention of punishing them; and, as for Brownie, it was impossible to catch him. So nobody was punished at all.

BROWNIE IN THE FARMYARD

Which was a place where he did not often go, for he preferred being warm and snug in the house. But when he felt himself ill-used, he would wander anywhere, in order to play tricks upon those whom he thought had done him harm; for, being only a Brownie and not a man, he did not understand that the best way to revenge yourself upon your enemies is either to let them alone or to pay them back good for evil—it disappoints them so much and makes them so exceedingly ashamed of themselves.

One day Brownie overheard the gardener advising the cook to put sour milk in his bowl at night, instead of sweet.

"He'd never find out the difference, no more than the pigs do. Indeed, it's my belief that a pig, or dog, or something, empties the bowl, and not a Brownie at all. It's just clean waste —that's what I say."

"Then you'd better hold your tongue and mind your own business," returned the cook, who was of a sharp temper and would not stand being meddled with. She began to abuse the gardener soundly; but his wife, who was standing by, took his part, as she always did when any third party scolded him. So they all squabbled together, till Brownie, hid under his coal, put his little hands over his little ears.

"Dear me, what a noise these mortals do make when they quarrel! They quite deafen me. I must teach them better manners."

But when the cook slammed the door to and left the gardener and his wife alone, they too began to dispute between themselves.

"You make such a fuss over your nasty pigs, and get all the scraps for them," said the wife. "It's of much more importance that I should have everything cook can spare for my chickens. Never were such fine chickens as my last brood."

"I thought they were ducklings."

"How you catch me up, you rude old man! They are ducklings, and beauties, too—even though they have never seen water. Where's the pond you promised to make for me, I wonder?"

"Rubbish, woman! If my cows do without a pond, your ducklings may. And why will you be so silly as to rear ducklings at all? Fine fat chickens are a deal better. You'll find out your mistake some day."

"And so will you when that old Alderney runs dry. You'll wish you had taken my advice, and fattened and sold her."

"Alderney cows won't sell for fattening, and women's advice is never worth twopence. Yours isn't worth even a halfpenny. What are you laughing at?"

"I wasn't laughing," said the wife angrily; and in truth it was not she, but little Brownie, running under the barrow which the gardener was wheeling along, and very much amused that people should be so silly as to squabble about nothing.

It was still early morning; for, whatever this old couple's faults might be, laziness was not one of them. The wife rose with the dawn to feed her poultry and collect her eggs; the husband also got through as much work by breakfast-time as many an idle man does by noon. But Brownie had been beforehand with them this day.

When all the fowls came running to be fed, the big Brahma

hen that had hatched the ducklings was seen wandering for-
lornly about and clucking mournfully for her young brood—
she could not find them anywhere. Had she been able to speak,
she might have told how a large white Aylesbury duck had waddled into the farmyard, and waddled out again, coaxing them
after her, no doubt in search of a pond. But missing they were,
most certainly.

"Cluck! cluck! cluck!" mourned the miserable hen-mother
—and, "Oh, my ducklings, my ducklings!" cried the gardener's
wife. "Who can have carried off my beautiful ducklings?"

"Rats, maybe," said the gardener cruelly as he walked away.
And as he went he heard the squeak of a rat below his wheel-
barrow. But he could not catch it any more than his wife could
catch the Aylesbury duck. Of course not. Both were—the
Brownie!

Just at this moment the six little people came running into
the farmyard. When they had been particularly good, they
were sometimes allowed to go with gardener a-milking, each
carrying his or her own mug for a drink of milk, warm from
the cow. They scampered after him—a noisy tribe, begging to
be taken down to the field, and holding out their six mugs entreatingly.

"What! Six cupfuls of milk, when I haven't a drop to spare
and cook is always wanting more? Ridiculous nonsense! Get
along with you; you may come to the field—I can't hinder that
—but you'll get no milk this day. Take your mugs back again
to the kitchen."

The poor little folks made the best of a bad business, and
obeyed; then followed the gardener down to the field rather
dolefully. But it was such a beautiful morning that they soon
recovered their spirits. The grass shone with dew, like a sheet

of diamonds, the clover smelled so sweet, and two skylarks were singing at one another high up in the sky. Several rabbits darted past, to their great amusement, especially one very large rabbit —brown, not gray—which dodged them in and out, and once nearly threw the gardener down, pail and all, by running across his feet; which set them all laughing, till they came where Dolly, the cow, lay chewing the cud under a large oak tree.

It was great fun to stir her up, as usual, and lie down, one after the other, in the place where she had lain all night long, making the grass flat, and warm, and perfumy with her sweet breath. She let them do it, and then stood meekly by; for Dolly was the gentlest cow in the world.

But this morning something strange seemed to possess her. She altogether refused to be milked—kicked, plunged, tossed over the pail, which was luckily empty.

"Bless the cow! What's wrong with her? It's surely you children's fault. Stand off, the whole lot of you. Soh, Dolly! Good Dolly!"

But Dolly was anything but good. She stood switching her tail and looking as savage as so mild an animal possibly could look.

"It's all your doing, you naughty children! You have been playing her some trick, I know," cried the gardener in great wrath.

They assured him they had done nothing, and, indeed, they looked as quiet as mice and as innocent as lambs. At length the biggest boy pointed out a large wasp which had settled in Dolly's ear.

"That accounts for everything," said the gardener.

But it did not mend everything; for when he tried to drive it away it kept on coming back and back again, and buzzing round his own head and the cow's, with a voice that the children thought was less like the buzz of a wasp than the sound of a person laughing. At length it frightened Dolly to such an extent that with one wild bound she darted right away, and galloped off to the further end of the field.

"I'll get a rope and tie her legs together," cried the gardener fiercely. "She shall repent giving me all this trouble—that she shall!"

"Ha! ha! ha!" laughed somebody. The gardener thought it was the children, and gave one of them an angry cuff as he walked away. But they knew it was somebody else, and were not at all surprised when, the minute his back was turned, Dolly came walking quietly back, led by a little wee brown man who scarcely reached up to her knees. Yet she let him guide her, which he did as gently as possible, though the string he held her by was no thicker than a spider web, floating from one of her horns.

"Soh, Dolly! Good Dolly!" cried Brownie, mimicking the gardener's voice. "Now we'll see what we can do. I want my breakfast badly—don't you, little folks?"

Of course they did, for the morning air made them very hungry.

"Very well—wait a bit, though. Old people should be served first, you know. Besides, I want to go to bed."

Go to bed in the daylight! The children all laughed, and then looked quite shy and sorry, lest they might have seemed rude to the little Brownie. But he—he liked fun and never took offense when none was meant.

He placed himself on the milking-stool, which was so high that his little legs were dangling half-way down, and milked and milked—Dolly standing as still as possible—till he had filled the whole pail. Most astonishing cow! She gave as much as two cows; and such delicious milk as it was—all frothing and yellow —richer than even Dolly's milk had ever been before. The children's mouths watered for it, but not a word said they—even when, instead of giving it to them, Brownie put his own mouth to the pail, and drank and drank, till it seemed as if he were never going to stop. But it was decidedly a relief to them when he popped his head up again, and lo! the pail was as full as ever!

"Now, little ones, now's your turn. Where are your mugs?"

All answered mournfully, "We've got none. The gardener made us take them back again."

"Never mind—all right. Gather me half a dozen of the biggest buttercups you can find."

"What nonsense!" thought the children; but they did it. Brownie laid the flowers in a row upon the eldest girl's lap— blew upon them one by one, and each turned into the most beautiful golden cup that ever was seen!

"Now, then, every one take his own mug, and I'll fill it."

He milked away—each child got a drink, and then the cups were filled again. And all the while Dolly stood as quiet as possible—looking benignly round, as if she would be happy to supply milk to the whole parish, if the Brownie desired it.

"Soh, Dolly! Thank you, Dolly!" said he again, mimicking the gardener's voice, half-growling, half-coaxing. And while he spoke, the real voice was heard behind the hedge. There was a sound as of a great wasp flying away, which made Dolly prick up her ears and look as if the old savageness was coming back upon her. The children snatched up their mugs, but there was no need—they had all turned into buttercups again.

The gardener jumped over the stile, as cross as two sticks, with an old rope in his hand.

"Oh, what a bother I've had! Breakfast ready, and no milk yet—and such a row as they are making over those lost ducklings. Stand back, you children, and don't hinder me a minute. No use begging—not a drop of milk shall you get. Hillo, Dolly! Quiet, old girl!"

Quiet enough she was this time—but you might as well have milked a plaster cow in a London milk-shop. Not one ringing drop resounded against the empty pail; for when they peeped in, the children saw, to their amazement, that it was empty.

"The creature's bewitched!" cried the gardener in a great fury. "Or else somebody has milked her dry already. Have you done it? Or you?" he asked each of the children.

They might have said no—which was the literal truth—but then it would not have been the whole truth, for they knew quite well that Dolly had been milked, and also who had done it. And their mother had always taught them that to make a person believe a lie is nearly as bad as telling him one. Yet still they did not like to betray the kind little Brownie. Greatly puzzled, they hung their heads and said nothing.

"Look in your pail again," cried a voice from the other side of Dolly. And there at the bottom was just the usual quantity of milk—no more and no less.

The gardener was very much astonished. "It must be the Brownie!" muttered he in a frightened tone; and taking off his hat, "Thank you, sir," said he to Mr. Nobody—at which the children all burst out laughing. But they kept their own counsel, and he was afraid to ask them any more questions.

By and by his fright wore off a little. "I only hope the milk is good milk, and will poison nobody," said he sulkily. "However, that's not my affair. You children had better tell your mother all about it. I left her in the farmyard in a pretty state of mind about her ducklings."

Perhaps Brownie heard this and was sorry, for he liked the children's mother, who had always been kind to him. Besides, he never did anybody harm who did not deserve it; and though, being a Brownie, he could hardly be said to have a conscience, he had something which stood in the place of one—a liking to see people happy rather than miserable.

So, instead of going to bed under his big coal for the day, when after breakfast the children and their mother came out to look at a new brood of chickens, he crept after them and hid behind the hen-coop where the old mother-hen was put, with her young ones round her.

There had been great difficulty in getting her in there, for she was a hen who hatched her brood on independent principles. Instead of sitting upon the nice nest that the gardener made for her, she had twice gone into a little wood close by and made a nest for herself, which nobody could ever find; and where she hatched in secret, coming every second day to be fed, and then vanishing again, till at last she reappeared in triumph, with her chickens running after her. The first brood there had been twelve, but of this there were fourteen—all from her own eggs, of course, and she was uncommonly proud of them. So was the gardener, so was the mistress—who liked all young things. Such a picture as they were! Fourteen soft, yellow, fluffy things, running about after their mother. It had been a most troublesome business to catch—first her, and then them, to put them under the coop. The old hen resisted, and pecked furiously at the gardener's legs, and the chickens ran about in frantic terror, chirping wildly in answer to her clucking.

At last, however, the little family was safe in shelter, and the chickens counted over, to see that none had been lost in the scuffle. How funny they were, looking so innocent and yet so wise, as chickens do—peering out at the world from under their mother's wing, or hopping over her back, or snuggled all together under her breast, so that nothing was seen of them but a mass of yellow legs, like a great centipede.

"How happy the old hen is," said the children's mother, looking on, and then looking compassionately at that other forlorn old hen, who had hatched the ducklings, and kept wandering about the farmyard, clucking miserably, "Those poor ducklings, what can have become of them? If rats had killed them, we should have found feathers or something; and weasels would have sucked their brains and left them. They must have been stolen, or wandered away, and died of cold and hunger—my poor ducklings!"

The mistress sighed, for she could not bear any living thing to suffer. And the children nearly cried at the thought of what might be happening to their pretty ducklings. That very minute a little wee brown face peeped through a hole in the hencoop, making the old mother-hen fly furiously at it—as she did at the slightest shadow of an enemy to her little ones. However, no harm happened—only a guinea-fowl suddenly ran across the farmyard, screaming in its usual harsh voice. But it was not the usual sort of guinea-fowl, being larger and handsomer than any of theirs.

"Oh, what a beauty of a creature! How did it ever come into our farmyard?" cried the delighted children; and started off after it, to catch it if possible.

But they ran, and they ran—through the gate and out into the lane; and the guinea-fowl still ran on before them, until, turning round a corner, they lost sight of it, and immediately saw something else, equally curious. Sitting on the top of a big thistle—so big that he must have had to climb it just like a tree —was the Brownie. His legs were crossed, and his arms too; his little brown cap was stuck knowingly on one side, and he was laughing heartily.

"How do you do? Here I am again. I thought I wouldn't go to bed, after all. Shall I help you to find the ducklings? Very well! Come along."

They crossed the field, Brownie running beside them, and as fast as they could, though he looked such an old man; and sometimes turning over on legs and arms like a Catherine wheel—which they tried to imitate, but generally failed, and only bruised their fingers and noses.

He lured them on and on till they came to the wood, and to a green path in it, which, well as they knew the neighborhood, none of the children had ever seen before. It led to a most beautiful pond, as clear as crystal and as blue as the sky. Large trees grew round it, dipping their branches in the water, as if they were looking at themselves in a glass. And all about their roots were quantities of primroses—the biggest primroses the little girls had ever seen. Down they dropped on their fat knees, squashing down more primroses than they gathered, though they tried to gather them all; and the smallest child ever began to cry because her hands were so full that the flowers dropped through her fingers. But the boys, older and more practical, rather despised primroses.

"I thought we had come to look for ducklings," said the eldest. "Mother is fretting dreadfully about them. Where can they be?"

"Shut your eyes, and you'll see," said the Brownie, at which

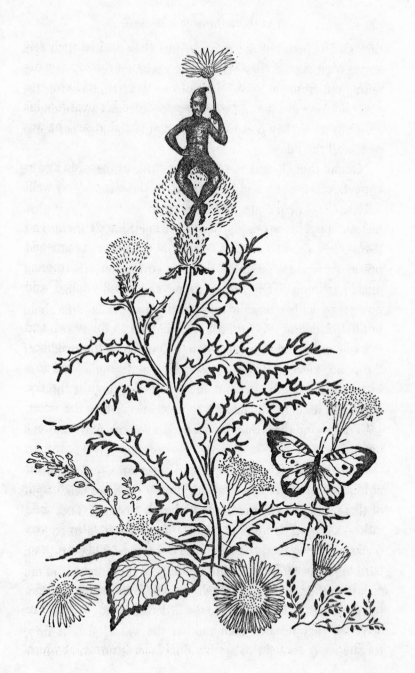

they all laughed, but did it, and when they opened their eyes again, what should they behold but a whole fleet of ducklings sailing out from the roots of an old willow tree, one after the other, looking as fat and content as possible, and swimming as naturally as if they had lived on a pond—and this particular pond—all their days.

"Count them," said the Brownie, "the whole eight—quite correct. And then try and catch them—if you can."

Easier said than done. The boys set to work with great satisfaction—boys do so enjoy hunting something. They coaxed them—they shouted at them—they threw little sticks at them; but as soon as they wanted them to go one way the fleet of ducklings immediately turned round and sailed another way, doing it so deliberately and majestically that the children could not help laughing. As for little Brownie, he sat on a branch of the willow tree, with his legs dangling down to the surface of the pond, kicking at the water-spiders, and grinning with all his might. At length, tired out, in spite of their fun, the children begged for his help, and he took compassion on them.

"Turn round three times and see what you can find," shouted he.

Immediately each little boy found in his arms, and each little girl in her pinafore, a fine fat duckling. And there being eight of them, the two elder children had each a couple. They were rather cold and damp, and slightly uncomfortable to cuddle, ducks not being used to cuddling. Poor things! They struggled hard to get away. But the children hugged them tight, and ran as fast as they could go through the wood, forgetting, in their joy, even to say "Thank you" to the little Brownie.

When they reached their mother she was as glad as they, for she never thought to see her ducklings again; and to have them back all alive and uninjured, and watch them running to the old hen, was so exciting that nobody thought of asking a single question as to where they had been found.

When the mother did ask, the children told her all about Brownie's taking them to the beautiful pond—and what a wonderful pond it was; how green the trees were round it; and how large the primroses grew. They never tired of talking about it and seeking for it. But the odd thing was that, seek as they might, they never could find it again. Many a day did the little people roam about one by one, or all together, round the wood, and across the wood, and up and down the wood, often getting themselves sadly draggled with mud and torn with brambles —but the beautiful pond they never found again.

Nor did the ducklings, I suppose; for they wandered no more from the farmyard, to the old mother-hen's great content. They grew up into fat and respectable ducks—five white ones and three gray ones—waddling about, very content, though they never saw water, except the tank which was placed for them to paddle in. They lived a lazy, peaceful, pleasant life for a long time, and were at last killed and eaten with green peas, one after the other, to the family's great satisfaction, if not to their own.

BROWNIE'S RIDE

For the little Brownie, though not given to horsemanship, did once take a ride, and a very remarkable one it was. Shall I tell you all about it?

The six little children got a present of something they had longed for all their lives—a pony. Not a rocking-horse, but a real live pony—a Shetland pony, too, which had traveled all the way from the Shetland Isles to Devonshire—where everybody wondered at it, for such a creature had not been seen in the neighborhood for years and years. She was no bigger than a donkey, and her coat, instead of being smooth like a horse, was shaggy like a young bear's. She had a long tail, which had never been cut, and such a deal of hair in her mane and over her eyes that it gave her quite a fierce countenance. In fact, among the mild and tame Devonshire beasts, the little Shetland pony looked almost like a wild animal. But in reality she was the gentlest creature in the world. Before she had been many days with them she began to know the children quite well; followed them about, ate corn out of the bowl they held out to her; nay, one day, when the eldest little girl offered her bread-and-butter, she stooped her head and took it from the child's hand, just like a young lady. Indeed, Jess—that was her name—was altogether so lady-like in her behavior that more than once cook allowed her to walk in at the back door, when she stood politely warming her nose at the kitchen fire for a minute or two, then turned round and as politely walked out again. But she never did any mischief, and was so quiet and gentle a creature that she bade fair soon to become as great a pet in the household as the dog, the cat, the kittens, the puppies, the fowls, the ducks, the cow, the pig, and all the other members of the family.

The only one who disliked her and grumbled at her was the gardener. This was odd; because, though cross to children, the old man was kind to dumb beasts. Even his pig knew his voice, and grunted and held out his nose to be scratched; and he always gave each successive pig a name, Jack or Dick, and called them by it, and was quite affectionate to them, one after the other, until the very day that they were killed. But they were English pigs—and the pony was Scotch—and the Devonshire gardener hated everything Scotch, he said; besides, he was not used to groom's work, and the pony required such a deal of grooming on account of her long hair. More than once the gardener threatened to clip it short and turn her into a regular English pony, but the children were in such distress at this that the mistress and mother forbade any such spoiling of Jessie's personal appearance.

At length, to keep things smooth and to avoid the rough words and even blows which poor Jess sometimes got, they sought in the village for a boy to look after her, and found a great rough, shock-headed lad named Bill, who for a few shillings a week consented to come up every morning and learn the beginning of a groom's business; hoping to end, as his mother said he should, in sitting, like the squire's fat coachman, as broad as he was long, on the top of the hammer-cloth of a grand carriage, and do nothing all day but drive a pair of horses as stout as himself a few miles along the road and back again.

Bill would have liked this very much, he thought, if he could have been a coachman all at once, for if there was one thing he disliked, it was work. He much preferred to lie in the sun all day and do nothing; and he only agreed to come and take care of Jess because she was such a very little pony that looking after her seemed next door to doing nothing. But when he tried it, he found his mistake. True, Jess was a very gentle beast; so quiet that the old mother-hen with fourteen chicks used, instead of roosting with the rest of the fowls, to come regularly into the portion of the cow-shed which was partitioned off for a stable and settle under a corner of Jess' manger for the night; and in the morning the chicks would be seen running about fearlessly among her feet and under her very nose.

But, for all that, she required a little management, for she did not like her long hair to be roughly handled; it took a long time to clean her; and, though she did not scream out like some silly little children when her hair was combed, I am afraid she sometimes kicked and bounced about, giving Bill a deal of trouble—all the more trouble the more impatient Bill was.

And then he had to keep within call, for the children wanted their pony at all hours. She was their own especial property, and they insisted upon learning to ride—even before they got a saddle. Hard work it was to stick on Jess' bare back, but by degrees the boys did it, turn and turn about, and even gave their sisters a turn too—a very little one—just once round the field and back again, which was quite enough, they considered, for girls. But they were very kind to their little sisters, held them on so that they could not fall, and led Jess carefully and quietly: and altogether behaved as elder brothers should.

Nor did they squabble very much among themselves, though sometimes it was rather difficult to keep their turns all fair, and remember accurately which was which. But they did their best, being on the whole extremely good children. And they were so happy to have their pony that they would have been ashamed to quarrel over her.

Also, one very curious thing kept them on their good behavior. Whenever they did begin to misconduct themselves— to want to ride out of their turns, or to domineer over one another, or the boys, joining together, tried to domineer over the girls, as I grieve to say boys not seldom do—they used to hear in the air, right over their heads, the crack of an unseen whip. It was none of theirs, for they had not got a whip; that was a felicity which their father had promised when they could all ride like young gentlemen and ladies; but there was no mistaking the sound—indeed, it always startled Jess so that she set off galloping, and could not be caught again for many minutes.

This happened several times, until one of them said, "Perhaps it's the Brownie." Whether it was or not, it made them behave better for a good while; till one unfortunate day the two eldest began contending which should ride foremost and which hindmost on Jess' back, when "Crick—crack!" went the whip in the air, frightening the pony so much that she kicked up her heels, tossed both the boys over her head, and scampered off, followed by a loud "Ha! ha! ha!"

It certainly did not come from the two boys, who had fallen —quite safely, but rather unpleasantly—into a large nettle-bed; whence they crawled out, rubbing their arms and legs, and looking too much ashamed to complain. But they were rather frightened and a little cross, for Jess took a skittish fit, and refused to be caught and mounted again, till the bell rang for school —when she grew as meek as possible. Too late—for the children were obliged to run indoors, and got no more rides for the whole day.

Jess was from this incident supposed to be on the same friendly terms with Brownie as were the rest of the household. Indeed, when she came, the children had taken care to lead her up to the coal-cellar door and introduce her properly—for they knew Brownie was very jealous of strangers, and often played them tricks. But after that piece of civility he would be sure, they thought, to take her under his protection. And sometimes, when the little Shetlander was restless and pricked up her ears, looking preternaturally wise under those shaggy brows of hers, the children used to say to one another, "Perhaps she sees the Brownie."

Whether she did or not, Jess sometimes seemed to see a good deal that others did not see, and was apparently a favorite with the Brownie, for she grew and thrived so much that she soon became the pride and delight of the children and of the whole family. You would hardly have known her for the rough, shaggy, half-starved little beast that had arrived a few weeks before. Her coat was so silky, her limbs so graceful, and her head so full of intelligence that everybody admired her. Then, even the gardener began to admire her too.

"I think I'll get upon her back; it will save me walking down to the village," said he, one day. And she actually carried him —though, as his feet nearly touched the ground, it looked as if the man were carrying the pony, and not the pony the man. And the children laughed so immoderately that he never tried it afterward.

Nor Bill neither, though he had once thought he should like a ride, and got astride on Jess; but she quickly ducked her head down, and he tumbled over it. Evidently she had her own tastes as to her riders, and much preferred little people to big ones.

Pretty Jess! When cantering round the paddock with the

young folk, she really was quite a picture. And when at last she got a saddle—a new, beautiful saddle, with a pommel to take off and on, so as to suit both boys and girls—how proud they all were, Jess included! That day they were allowed to take her into the market-town—the gardener leading her, as Bill could not be trusted—and everybody, even the blacksmith, who hoped by and by to have the pleasure of shoeing her, said what a beautiful pony she was!

After this, the gardener treated Jess a great deal better, and showed Bill how to groom her, and kept him close at it too, which Bill did not like at all. He was a very lazy lad, and whenever he could shirk work he did it; and many a time when the children wanted Jess, either there was nobody to saddle her or she had not been properly groomed, or Bill was away at his dinner, and they had to wait till he came back and could put her in order to be taken out for a ride like a genteel animal— which I am afraid neither pony nor children enjoyed half so much as the old ways before Bill came.

Still, they were gradually becoming excellent little horsemen and horsewomen—even the youngest, only four years old, whom all the rest were very tender over and who was often held on Jess' back and given a ride out of her turn because she was a good little girl and never cried for it. And seldomer and seldomer was heard the mysterious sound of the whip in the air, which warned them of quarreling—Brownie hated quarreling.

In fact, their only trouble was Bill, who never came to his work in time, and never did things when wanted, and was ill-natured, lazy, and cross to the children, so that they disliked him very much.

"I wish the Brownie would punish you," said one of the boys; "you'd behave better then."

"The Brownie!" cried Bill contemptuously. "If I caught him, I'd kick him up in the air like this!"

And he kicked up his cap—his only cap, it was—which, strange to relate, flew right up, ever so high, and lodged at the very top of a tree which overhung the stable, where it dangled for weeks and weeks, during which time poor Bill had to go bareheaded.

He was very much vexed, and revenged himself by vexing the children in all sorts of ways. They would have told their mother and asked her to send Bill away, only she had a great many anxieties just then, for their dear old grandmother was very ill, and they did not like to make a fuss about anything that would trouble her.

So Bill stayed on, and nobody found out what a bad, ill-natured, lazy boy he was.

But one day the mother was sent for suddenly, not knowing when she should be able to come home again. She was very sad and so were the children, for they loved their grandmother —and as the carriage drove off they all stood crying round the front door for ever so long.

The servants even cried too—all but Bill.

"It's an ill wind that blows nobody good," said he. "What a jolly time I shall have! I'll do nothing all day long. Those troublesome children shan't have Jess to ride; I'll keep her in the stable, and then she won't get dirty, and I shall have no trouble in cleaning her. Hurrah! What fun!"

He put his hands in his pockets, and sat whistling the best part of the afternoon.

The children had been so unhappy that for that day they

quite forgot Jess; but next morning after lessons were over they came begging for a ride.

"You can't get one. The stable door's locked, and I've lost the key." (He had it in his pocket all the time.)

"How is poor Jess to get her dinner?" cried a thoughtful little girl. "How hungry she will be!"

And the child was quite in distress, as were the two other girls. But the boys were more angry than sorry.

"It was very stupid of you, Bill, to lose the key. Look about and find it, or else break open the door."

"I won't," said Bill; "I dare say the key will turn up before night, and if it doesn't, who cares? You get riding enough and too much. I'll not bother myself about it, or Jess either."

And Bill sauntered away. He was a big fellow, and the little lads were rather afraid of him. But as he walked, he could not keep his hand out of his trousers pocket, where the key felt growing heavier and heavier, till he expected it every minute to tumble through and come out at his boots—convicting him before all the children of having told a lie.

Nobody was in the habit of telling lies to them, so they never suspected him, but went innocently searching about for the key—Bill all the while clutching it fast. But every time he touched it, he felt his fingers pinched, as if there was a cockroach in his pocket—or a little lobster—or something, anyhow, that had claws. At last, fairly frightened, he made an excuse to go into the cow-shed, took the key out of his pocket and looked at it, and finally hid it in a corner of the manger, among the hay.

As he did so, he heard a most extraordinary laugh, which was certainly not from Dolly the cow, and, as he went out of the shed, he felt the same sort of pinch at his ankles, which made him so angry that he kept striking with his whip in all directions, but hit nobody, for nobody was there.

But Jess—who, as soon as she heard the children's voices, had set up a most melancholy whinnying behind the locked stable-door—began to neigh energetically. And Boxer barked, and the hens cackled, and the guinea-fowls cried, "Come back, come back!" in their usual insane fashion—indeed, the whole farm-yard seemed in such an excited state that the children got frightened lest the gardener should scold them, and ran away, leaving Bill master of the field.

What an idle day he had! How he sat on the wall with his hands in his pockets, and lounged upon the fence, and saun-tered round the garden! At length, absolutely tired of doing nothing, he went and talked with the gardener's wife while she was hanging out her clothes. The gardener had gone down to the lower field, with all the little folks after him, so that he knew nothing of Bill's idling, or it might have come to an end.

By and by Bill thought it was time to go home to his sup-per. "But first I'll give Jess her corn," said he, "double quantity, and then I need not come back to give her her breakfast so early in the morning. Soh, you greedy beast! I'll be at you pres-ently, if you don't stop that noise."

For Jess, at the sound of his footsteps, was heard to whinny in the most imploring manner, enough to have melted a heart of stone.

"The key—where on earth did I put the key?" cried Bill, whose constant habit it was to lay things out of his hand and then forget where he had put them, causing himself endless loss of time in searching for them—as now. At last he suddenly re-membered the corner of the cow's manger, where he felt sure he had left it. But the key was not there.

"You can't have eaten it, you silly old cow," said he, striking Dolly on the nose as she rubbed herself against him—she was an affectionate beast. "Nor you, you stupid old hen!" kicking the mother of the brood, who with her fourteen chicks being shut out of their usual roosting-place—Jess' stable—kept pecking about under Dolly's legs. "It can't have gone without hands— of course it can't." But most certainly the key was gone.

What in the world should Bill do? Jess kept on making a pitiful complaining. No wonder, as she had not tasted food since morning. It would have made any kind-hearted person quite sad to hear her, thinking how exceedingly hungry the poor pony must be.

Little did Bill care for that, or for anything, except that he should be sure to get into trouble as soon as he was found out. When he heard the gardener coming into the farmyard, with the children after him, Bill bolted over the wall like a flash of lightning, and ran away home, leaving poor Jess to her fate.

All the way he seemed to hear at his heels a little dog yelping, and then a swarm of gnats buzzing round his head, and altogether was so perplexed and bewildered that when he got into his mother's cottage he escaped into bed, and pulled the blanket over his ears to shut out the noise of the dog and the gnats, which at last turned into a sound like somebody laughing. It was not his mother, she didn't often laugh, poor soul! Bill bothered her quite too much for that, and he knew it. Dreadfully frightened, he hid his head under the bed-clothes, determined to go to sleep and think about nothing till next day.

Meantime the gardener returned, with all the little people trooping after him. He had been rather kinder to them than usual this day, because he knew their mother had gone away in trouble, and now he let them help him to roll the gravel, and fetch up Dolly to be milked, and watch him milk her in the cow-shed—where, it being nearly winter, she always spent the night now. They were so well amused that they forgot all about their disappointment as to the ride, and Jess did not remind them of it by her whinnying. For as soon as Bill was gone she grew quite silent.

At last one little girl, the one who had cried over Jess' being left hungry, remembered the poor pony, and peeping through a crevice in the cow-shed, saw her stand contentedly munching at a large bowlful of corn.

"So Bill did find the key. I'm very glad," thought the kind little maiden, and to make sure looked again, when—what do you think she beheld squatting on the manger? Something brown—either a large brown rat or a small brown man. But she held her tongue, since, being a very little girl, people sometimes laughed at her for the strange things she saw. She was quite certain she did see them, for all that.

So she and the rest of the children went indoors and to bed. When they were fast asleep, something happened. Something so curious that the youngest boy, who, thinking he heard Jess neighing, got up to look out, was afraid to tell, lest he too should be laughed at, and went back to bed immediately.

In the middle of the night a little old brown man carrying a lantern, or at least having a light in his hand that looked like a lantern, went and unlocked Jess' stable, and patted her pretty head. At first she started, but soon she grew quiet and pleased and let him do what he chose with her. He began rubbing her down, making the same funny hissing with his mouth that Bill did, and all grooms do—I never could find out why. But Jess evidently liked it, and stood as good as possible.

"Isn't it nice to be clean?" said the wee man, talking to her as if she were a human being or a Brownie. "And I dare say your poor little legs ache with standing still so long. Shall we have a run together? The moon shines bright in the clear, cold night. Dear me! I'm talking poetry."

But Brownies are not poetical fairies quite commonplace, and up to all sorts of work. So, while he talked, he was saddling and bridling Jess, she not objecting in the least. Finally he jumped on her back.

" 'Off, said the stranger—off, off, and away,' " sang Brownie, mimicking a song of the cook's. People in that house often heard their songs repeated in the oddest way, from room to room, everybody fancying it was somebody else that did it. But it was only the Brownie. "Now, 'A southerly wind and a cloudy sky proclaim it a hunting morning!' "

Or night—for it was the middle of the night, though bright as day—and Jess galloped and the Brownie sat on her back as merrily as if they had gone hunting together all their days.

Such a steeplechase it was! They cleared the farmyard at a single bound, and went flying down the road, and across the plowed field, and into the wood. Then out in the open country, and by and by into a dark, muddy lane—and oh! how muddy Devonshire lanes can be sometimes!

"Let's go into the water to wash ourselves," said Brownie, and coaxed Jess into a deep stream, which she swam as bravely as possible—she had not had such a frolic since she left her native Shetland Isles. Up the bank she scrambled, her long hair dripping as if she had been a water-dog instead of a pony. Brownie, too, shook himself like a rat or a beaver, throwing a shower round him in all directions.

"Never mind; at it again, my lass!" and he urged Jess into

the water once more. Out she came, wetter and brisker than ever, and went back home through the lane, and the wood, and the plowed field, galloping like the wind, and tossing back her ears and mane and tail, perfectly frantic with enjoyment.

But when she reached her stable, the plight she was in would have driven any respectable groom frantic too. Her sides were white with foam, and the mud was sticking all over her like a plaster. As for her beautiful long hair, it was all caked together in a tangle, as if all the combs in the world would never make it smooth again. Her mane especially was plaited into knots, which people in Devonshire call elf-locks, and say, when they find them on their horses, that it is because the fairies have been riding them.

Certainly poor Jess had been pretty well ridden that night! When, just as the dawn began to break, the gardener got up and looked into the farmyard, his sharp eye caught sight of the stable-door, wide open.

"Well done, Bill," shouted he; "up early at last. One hour before breakfast is worth three after."

But no Bill was there; only Jess, trembling and shaking, all in a foam, and muddy from head to foot, but looking perfectly cheerful in her mind. And out from under her fore legs ran a small creature, which the gardener mistook for Tiny, only Tiny was gray, and this dog was brown, of course!

I should not like to tell you all that was said to Bill when, an hour after breakfast-time, he came skulking up to the farm. In fact, words failing, the gardener took a good stick and laid it about Bill's shoulders, saying he would either do this or tell the mistress of him, and how he had left the stable-door open all night, and some bad fellow had stolen Jess, and galloped her all across the country, till, if she hadn't been the cleverest pony in the world, she never could have got back again.

Bill durst not contradict this explanation of the story, especially as the key was found hanging up in its proper place by the kitchen-door. And when he went to fetch it, he heard the most extraordinary sound in the coal-cellar close by—like somebody snoring or laughing. Bill took to his heels and did not come back for a whole hour.

But when he did come back, he made himself as busy as possible. He cleaned Jess, which was half a day's work at least. Then he took the little people a ride, and afterward put his stable in the most beautiful order, and altogether was such a changed Bill that the gardener told him he must have left himself at home and brought back somebody else: whether or not, the boy certainly improved, so that there was less occasion to find fault with him afterward.

Jess lived to be quite an old pony, and carried a great many people—little people always, for she herself never grew any bigger. But I don't think she ever carried a Brownie again.

BROWNIE ON THE ICE

Winter was a grand time with the six little children, especially when they had frost and snow. This happened seldom enough for it to be the greatest possible treat when it did happen; and it never lasted very long, for the winters are warm in Devonshire.

There was a little lake three fields off, which made the most splendid sliding-place imaginable. No skaters went near it—it was not large enough; and besides, there was nobody to skate, the neighborhood being lonely. The lake itself looked the loneliest place imaginable. It was not very deep—not deep enough to drown a man—but it had a gravelly bottom, and was always very clear. Also, the trees round it grew so thick that they sheltered it completely from the wind; so, when it did freeze, it generally froze as smooth as a sheet of glass.

"The lake bears!" was such a grand event, and so rare, that when it did occur the news came at once to the farm, and the children carried it as quickly to their mother. For she had promised them that, if such a thing did happen this year—it did not happen every year—lessons should be stopped entirely and they should all go down to the lake and slide, if they liked, all day long.

So one morning, just before Christmas, the eldest boy ran in with a countenance of great delight.

"Mother, mother, the lake bears!" (It was rather a compliment to call it a lake, it being only about twenty yards across and forty long.) "The lake really bears!"

"Who says so?"

"Bill. Bill has been on it for an hour this morning, and has made us two such beautiful slides, he says—an up-slide and a down-slide. May we go to them directly?"

The mother hesitated.

"You promised, you know," pleaded the children.

"Very well, then; only be careful."

"And may we slide all day long, and never come home for dinner or anything?"

"Yes, if you like. Only the gardener must go with you, and stay all day."

This they did not like at all; nor, when the gardener was spoken to, did he.

"You bothering children! I wish you may all get a good ducking in the lake! Serve you right for making me lose a day's work, just to look after you little monkeys. I've a great mind to tell your mother I won't do it."

But he did not, being fond of his mistress. He was also fond of his work, but he had no notion of play. I think the saying of "All work and no play makes Jack a dull boy" must have been applied to him, for the gardener, whatever he had been as a boy, was certainly a dull and melancholy man. The children used to say that if he and idle Bill could have been kneaded into one, and baked in the oven—a very warm oven—they would have come out rather a pleasant person.

As it was, the gardener was anything but a pleasant person; above all, to spend a long day with, and on the ice, where one needs all one's cheerfulness and good-humor to bear pinched fingers and numbed toes, and trips and tumbles, and various uncomfortablenesses.

"He'll growl at us all day long—he'll be a regular spoil-sport!" lamented the children. "Oh! mother, mightn't we go alone?"

"No!" said the mother; and her "No" meant no, though she was always very kind. They argued the point no more, but started off, rather downhearted. But soon they regained their spirits, for it was a bright, clear, frosty day—the sun shining, though not enough to melt the ice, and just sufficient to lie like a thin sprinkling over the grass, and turn the brown branches into white ones. The little people danced along to keep themselves warm, carrying between them a basket which held their lunch. A very harmless lunch it was—just a large brown loaf and a lump of cheese, and a knife to cut it with. Tossing the basket about in their fun, they managed to tumble the knife out, and were having a search for it in the long grass, when the gardener came up, grumpily enough.

"To think of trusting you children with one of the table-knives and a basket! What a fool cook must be! I'll tell her so; and if they're lost she'll blame me: give me the things."

He put the knife angrily in one pocket. "Perhaps it will cut a hole in it," said one of the children, in rather a plèased tone than otherwise; then he turned the lunch all out on the grass and crammed it in the other pocket, hiding the basket behind a hedge.

"I'm sure I'll not be at the trouble of carrying it," said he, when the children cried out at this; "and you shan't carry it either, for you'll knock it about and spoil it. And as for your lunch getting warm in my pocket, why, so much the better this cold day."

It was not a lively joke, and they knew his pocket was very

dirty; indeed, the little girls had seen him stuff a dead rat into it only the day before. They looked ready to cry; but there was no help for them, except going back and complaining to their mother, and they did not like to do that. Besides, they knew that, though the gardener was cross, he was trustworthy, and she would never let them go down to the lake without him.

So they followed him, trying to be as good as they could—though it was difficult work. One of them proposed pelting him with snowballs, as they pelted each other. But at the first—which fell in his neck—he turned round so furiously that they never sent a second, but walked behind him as meek as mice.

As they went they heard little steps pattering after them.

"Perhaps it is the Brownie coming to play with us—I wish he would," whispered the youngest girl to the eldest boy, whose hand she generally held; and then the little pattering steps sounded again, traveling through the snow, but they saw nobody—so they said nothing.

The children would have liked to go straight to the ice; but the gardener insisted on taking them a mile round, to look at an extraordinary animal which a farmer there had just got—sent by his brother in Australia. The two old men stood gossiping so long that the children wearied extremely. Every minute seemed an hour till they got on the ice.

At last one of them pulled the gardener's coat-tails, and whispered that they were quite ready to go.

"Then I'm not," and he waited ever so much longer, and got a drink of hot cider, which made him quite lively for a little while.

But by the time they reached the lake, he was as cross as ever. He struck the ice with his stick, but made no attempt to see if it really did bear—though he would not allow the children to go one step upon it till he had tried.

"I know it doesn't bear, and you'll just have to go home again —a good thing too—saves me from losing a day's work."

"Try, only try; Bill said it bore," implored the boys, and looked wistfully at the two beautiful slides—just as Bill said, one up and one down—stretching all across the lake; "of course it bears, or Bill could not have made these slides."

"Bill's an ass!" said the gardener, and put his heavy foot cautiously on the ice. Just then there was seen jumping across it a creature which certainly had never been seen on the ice before. It made the most extraordinary bounds on its long hind legs, with its little fore legs tucked up in front of it as if it wanted to carry a muff; and its long, stiff tail sticking out straight behind, to balance itself with, apparently. The children at first started with surprise, and then burst out laughing, for it was the funniest creature, and had the funniest way of getting along, that they had ever seen in their lives.

"It's the kangaroo!" cried the gardener in great excitement. "It has got loose—and it's sure to be lost—and what a way Mr. Giles will be in! I must go and tell him. Or stop, I'll try and catch it."

But in vain—it darted once or twice across the ice, dodging him, as it were; and once coming so close that he nearly caught it by the tail—to the children's great delight—then it vanished entirely.

"I must go and tell Mr. Giles directly," said the gardener, and then stopped. For he had promised not to leave the children; and it was such a wild-goose chase, after an escaped kangaroo. But he might get half a crown as a reward, and he was sure of another glass of cider.

"You just stop quiet here, and I'll be back in five minutes," said he to the children. "You may go a little way on the ice—I think it's sound enough, only mind you don't tumble in, for there'll be nobody to pull you out."

"Oh, no," said the children, clapping their hands. They did not care for tumbling in, and were quite glad there was nobody there to pull them out. They hoped the gardener would stop a very long time away—only, as some one suggested when he was seen hurrying across the snowy field, he had taken away their lunch in his pocket, too.

"Never mind—we're not hungry yet. Now for a slide."

Off they darted, the three elder boys, with a good run; the biggest of the girls followed after them; and soon the whole four were skimming one after the other, as fast as a railway train, across the slippery ice. And, like a railway train, they had a collision, and all came tumbling one over the other, with great screaming and laughter, to the high bank on the other side. The two younger ones stood mournfully watching the others from the opposite bank—when there stood beside them a small brown man.

"Ho-ho! little people," said he, coming between them and taking hold of a hand of each. His was so warm and theirs so cold that it was quite comfortable. And then, somehow, they found in their open mouths a nice lozenge—I think it was peppermint, but am not sure; which comforted them still more.

"Did you want me to play with you?" cried the Brownie. "Then here I am! What shall we do? Have a turn on the ice together?"

No sooner said than done. The two little children felt themselves floating along—it was more like floating than running—

with Brownie between them; up the lake, and down the lake, and across the lake, not at all interfering with the sliders—indeed, it was a great deal better than sliding. Rosy and breathless, their toes so nice and warm, and their hands feeling like mince-pies just taken out of the oven—the little ones came to a standstill.

The elder ones stopped their sliding and looked toward Brownie with entreating eyes. He swung himself up to a willow bough, and then turned head over heels on to the ice.

"Halloo! You don't mean to say you big ones want a race too! Well, come along—if the two eldest will give a slide to the little ones."

He watched them take a tiny sister between them, and slide her up one slide and down another, screaming with delight. Then he took the two middle children in either hand.

"One, two, three, and away!" Off they started—scudding along as light as feathers and as fast as steam-engines, over the smooth, black ice, so clear that they could see the bits of stick and water-grasses frozen in it, and even the little fishes swimming far down below—if they had only looked long enough.

When all had had their fair turns, they began to be frightfully hungry.

"Catch a fish for dinner, and I'll lend you a hook," said Brownie. At which they all laughed, and then looked rather grave. Pulling a cold, raw, live fish from under the ice and eating it was not a pleasant idea of dinner. "Well, what would you like to have? Let the little one choose."

She said, after thinking a minute, that she should like a currant-cake.

"And I'd give you all a bit of it—a very large bit—I would

indeed!" added she, almost with the tears in her eyes—she was so very hungry.

"Do it, then!" said the Brownie, in his little squeaking voice.

Immediately the stone that the little girl was sitting on—a round, hard stone, and so cold!—turned into a nice hot cake—so hot that she jumped up directly. As soon as she saw what it was, she clapped her hands for joy.

"Oh, what a beautiful, beautiful cake! Only we haven't got a knife to cut it."

The boys felt in all their pockets, but somehow their knives never were there when they were wanted.

"Look! You've got one in your hand!" said Brownie to the little one; and that minute a bit of stick she held turned into a bread-knife—silver, with an ivory handle—big enough and sharp enough, without being too sharp. For the youngest girl was not allowed to use sharp knives, though she liked cutting things excessively, especially cakes.

"That will do. Sit you down and carve the dinner. Fair shares, and don't let anybody eat too much. Now begin, ma'am," said the Brownie quite politely, as if she had been ever so old.

Oh, how proud the little girl was! How bravely she set to work, and cut five of the biggest slices you ever saw, and gave them to her brothers and sisters, and was just going to take the sixth slice for herself, when she remembered the Brownie.

"I beg your pardon," said she as politely as he, though she was such a very little girl, and turned round to the wee brown man. But he was nowhere to be seen. The slices of cake in the children's hands remained cake, and uncommonly good it was, and such substantial eating that it did nearly the same as dinner: but the cake itself turned suddenly to a stone again, and the knife into a bit of stick.

For there was the gardener coming clumping along by the bank of the lake, and growling as he went.

"Have you got the kangaroo?" shouted the children, determined to be civil, if possible.

"This place is bewitched, I think," said he. "The kangaroo was fast asleep in the cow-shed. What! How dare you laugh at me?"

But they hadn't laughed at all. And they found it no laughing matter, poor children, when the gardener came on the ice, and began to scold them and order them about. He was perfectly savage with crossness; for the people at Giles' farm had laughed at him very much, and he did not like to be laughed at—and at the top of the field he had by chance met his mistress, and she had asked him severely how he could think of leaving the children alone.

Altogether, his conscience pricked him a good deal; and when people's consciences prick them, sometimes they get angry with other people, which is very silly, and only makes matters worse.

"What have you been doing all this time?" said he.

"All this five minutes?" said the eldest boy mischievously; for the gardener was only to be away five minutes, and had stayed a full hour. Also, when he fumbled in his pocket for the children's lunch—to stop their tongues, perhaps—he found it was not there.

They set up a great outcry; for, in spite of the cake, they could have eaten a little more. Indeed, the frost had such an effect upon all their appetites that they felt not unlike that celebrated gentleman of whom it is told that,

"He ate a cow, and ate a calf,
He ate an ox, and ate a half;
He ate a church, he ate the steeple,
He ate the priest, and all the people,
And said he hadn't had enough then."

"We're so hungry, so very hungry! Couldn't you go back again and fetch us some dinner?" cried they entreatingly.

"Not I, indeed. You may go back to dinner yourselves. You shall, indeed, for I want my dinner too. Two hours is plenty long enough to stop on the ice."

"It isn't two hours—it's only one."

"Well, one will do better than more. You're all right now—and you might soon tumble in, or break your legs on the slide. So come away home."

It wasn't kind of the gardener, and I don't wonder the children felt it hard; indeed, the eldest boy resisted stoutly.

"Mother said we might stop all day, and we will stop all day. You may go home if you like."

"I won't and you shall!" said the gardener, smacking a whip that he carried in his hand. "Stop till I catch you, and I'll give you this about your back, my fine gentleman."

And he tried to follow, but the little fellow darted across the ice, objecting to be either caught or whipped. It may have been rather naughty, but I am afraid it was great fun dodging the gardener up and down; he being too timid to go on the slippery ice, and sometimes getting so close that the whip nearly touched the lad.

"Bless us! There's the kangaroo again!" said he, starting. Just as he had caught the boy and lifted the whip, the creature was seen hop-hopping from bank to bank. "I can't surely be mistaken this time; I must catch it."

Which seemed quite easy, for it limped as if it was lame, or as if the frost had bitten its toes, poor beast! The gardener went after it, walking cautiously on the slippery, crackling ice, and never minding whether or not he walked on the slides, though they called out to him that his nailed boots would spoil them.

But whether it was that ice which bears a boy will not bear a man, or whether at each lame step of the kangaroo there came a great crack, is more than I can tell. However, just as the gardener reached the middle of the lake, the ice suddenly broke, and in he popped. The kangaroo too, apparently, for it was not seen afterward.

What a hullabaloo the poor man made! Not that he was drowning—the lake was too shallow to drown anybody; but he got terribly wet, and the water was very cold. He soon scrambled out, the boys helping him; and then he hobbled home as fast as he could, not even saying thank you, or taking the least notice of them.

Indeed, nobody took any notice of them—nobody came to fetch them, and they might have stayed sliding the whole afternoon. Only somehow they did not feel quite easy in their minds. And though the hole in the ice closed up immediately, and it seemed as firm as ever, still they did not like to slide upon it again.

"I think we had better go home and tell mother everything," said one of them. "Besides, we ought to see what has become of the poor gardener. He was very wet."

"Yes; but oh, how funny he looked!" And they all burst out laughing at the recollection of the figure he cut, scrambling out through the ice with his trousers dripping up to the knees, and the water running out of his boots, making a little pool wherever he stepped.

"And it freezes so hard that by the time he gets home his clothes will be as stiff as a board. His wife will have to put him to the fire to thaw before he can get out of them."

Again the little people burst into shouts of laughter. Although they laughed, they were a little sorry for the poor old gardener, and hoped no great harm had come to him, but that he had got safe home and been dried by his own warm fire.

The frosty mist was beginning already to rise, and the sun, though still high up in the sky, looked like a ball of red-hot iron as the six children went homeward across the fields—merry enough still, but not quite so merry as they had been a few hours before.

"Let's hope mother won't be vexed with us," said they, "but will let us come back again tomorrow. It wasn't our fault the gardener tumbled in."

As somebody said this, they all heard quite distinctly, "Ha! ha! ha!" and "Ho! ho! ho!" and a sound of little steps pattering behind.

But whatever they thought, nobody ventured to say that it was the fault of the Brownie.

BROWNIE AND THE CLOTHES

Till the next time; but when there is a Brownie in the house, no one can say that any of his tricks will be the last. For there's no stopping a Brownie, and no getting rid of him either. This one had followed the family from house to house, generation after generation—never any older, and sometimes seeming even to grow younger, by the tricks he played. In fact, though he looked like an old man, he was a perpetual child.

To the children he never did any harm; quite the contrary. And his chief misdoings were against those who vexed the children. But he gradually made friends with several of his grown-up enemies. Cook, for instance, who had ceased to be lazy at night and late in the morning, found no more black foot-marks on her white table-cloth. And Brownie found his basin of milk waiting for him, night after night, behind the coal-cellar door.

Bill, too, got on well enough with his pony, and Jess was taken no more night-rides. No ducks were lost; and Dolly gave her milk quite comfortably to whoever milked her. Alas! this was either Bill or the gardener's wife now. After that adventure on the ice, the poor gardener very seldom appeared; when he did, it was on two crutches, for he had had rheumatism in his feet, and could not stir outside his cottage door. So Bill had double work which was probably better for Bill.

The garden had to take care of itself; but this being winter-time, it did not much signify. Besides, Brownie seldom went into the garden, except in summer; during the hard weather he preferred to stop in his coal-cellar. It might not have been a lively place, but it was warm, and he liked it.

He had company there, too; for when the cat had more kittens—the kitten he used to tease being grown up now—they were all put in a hamper in the coal-cellar; and of cold nights Brownie used to jump in beside them, and be as warm and as cozy as a kitten himself. The little things never were heard to mew; so it may be supposed they liked his society. And the old mother-cat evidently bore him no malice for the whipping she had got by mistake; so Brownie must have found means of coaxing her over. One thing you may be sure of—all the while she and her kittens were in his coal-cellar, he took care never to turn himself into a mouse.

He was spending the winter, on the whole, very comfortably, without much trouble either to himself or his neighbors, when one day, the coal-cellar being nearly empty, two men, and a great wagon-load of coals behind them, came to the door, the gardener's wife following.

"My man says you're to give the cellar a good cleaning out before you put any more in," said she in her sharp voice; "and don't be lazy about it. It'll not take you ten minutes, for it's nearly all coal-dust, except that one big lump in the corner— you might clear that out too."

"Stop, it's the Brownie's lump! Better not meddle with it," whispered the little scullery-maid.

"Don't you meddle with matters that can't concern you," said the gardener's wife, who had been thinking what a nice help it would be to her fire. To be sure, it was not her lump of coal, but she thought she might take it; the mistress would never miss it, or the Brownie either. He must be a very silly old Brownie to live under a lump of coal.

So she argued with herself, and made the men lift it. "You must lift it, you see, if you are to sweep the coal-cellar out clean. And you may as well put it on the barrow, and I'll wheel it out of your way."

This she said in quite a civil voice, lest they should tell of her, and stood by while it was being done. It was done without anything happening, except that a large rat ran out of the coal-cellar door, bouncing against her feet, and frightening her so much that she nearly tumbled down.

"See what nonsense it is to talk of Brownies living in a coal-cellar. Nothing lives there but rats, and I'll have them poisoned pretty soon, and get rid of them."

But she was rather frightened all the same, for the rat had been such a very big rat, and had looked at her, as it darted past, with such wild, bright, mischievous eyes—brown eyes, of course —that she all but jumped with surprise.

However, she had got her lump of coal, and was wheeling it quietly away, nobody seeing, to her cottage at the bottom of the garden. She was a hard-worked woman, and her husband's illness made things harder for her. Still, she was not quite easy at taking what did not belong to her.

"I don't suppose anybody will miss the coal," she repeated. "I dare say the mistress would have given it to me if I had asked her; and as for its being the Brownie's lump—fudge! Bless us! What's that?"

For the barrow began to creak dreadfully, and every creak sounded like the cry of a child, just as if the wheel were going over its leg and crushing its poor little bones.

"What a horrid noise! I must grease the barrow. If only I knew where they keep the grease-box. All goes wrong, now my old man's laid up. Oh, dear! oh, dear!"

For suddenly the barrow had tilted over, though there was not a single stone near, and the big coal was tumbled on to the ground, where it broke into a thousand pieces. Gathering it up again was hopeless, and it made such a mess on the gravel walk, that the old woman was thankful her misfortune happened behind the privet hedge, where nobody was likely to come.

"I'll take a broom and sweep it up to-morrow. Nobody goes near the orchard now, except me when I hang out the clothes; so I need say nothing about it to the old man or anybody. But ah! deary me, what a beautiful lot of coal I've lost!"

She stood and looked at it mournfully, and then went into her cottage, where she found two or three of the little children keeping the gardener company. They did not dislike to do this now; but he was so much kinder than he used to be—so quiet and patient, though he suffered very much. And he had never once reproached them for what they always remembered—how it was ever since he was on the ice with them that he had got the rheumatism.

So, one or other of them made a point of going to see him every day, and telling him all the funny things they could think of—indeed, it was a contest among them who should first make the gardener laugh. They did not succeed in doing that exactly; but they managed to make him smile; and he was always gentle and grateful to them; so that they sometimes thought it was rather nice his being ill.

But his wife was not pleasant; she grumbled all day long, and snapped at him and his visitors; being especially snappish this day, because she had lost her big coal.

"I can't have you children come bothering here," said she crossly. "I want to wring out my clothes and hang them to dry. Be off with you!"

"Let us stop a little—just to tell the gardener this one curious thing about Dolly and the pig—and then we'll help you to take your clothes to the orchard; we can carry your basket between us—we can, indeed."

That was the last thing the woman wished; for she knew that the children would be sure to see the mess on the gravel walk—and they were such inquisitive children—they noticed everything. They would want to know all about it, and how the bits of coal came there. It was a very awkward position. But people who take other people's property often do find themselves in awkward positions.

"Thank you, young gentlemen," said she quite politely; "but indeed the basket is too heavy for you. However, you may stop and gossip a little longer with my old man. He likes it."

And while they were shut up with the gardener in his bedroom, off she went, carrying the basket on her head, and hung her clothes carefully out—the big things on lines between the fruit-trees, and the little things, such as stockings and pocket-handkerchiefs, stuck on the gooseberry-bushes, or spread upon the clean green grass.

"Such a fine day as it is! They'll dry directly," said she cheerfully to herself. "Plenty of sun, and not a breath of wind to blow them about. I'll leave them for an hour or two, and come and fetch them in before it grows dark. Then I shall get all my folding done by bedtime, and have a clear day for ironing to-morrow."

But when she did fetch them in, having bundled them all together in the dusk of the evening, never was such a sight as those clothes! They were all twisted in the oddest way—the stockings turned inside out, with the heels and toes tucked into the legs; the sleeves of the shirts tied together in double knots, the pocket-handkerchiefs made into round balls, so tight that if you had pelted a person with them they would have given very hard blows indeed. And the whole looked as if, instead of lying quietly on the grass and bushes, they had been dragged through heaps of mud and then stamped upon, so that there was not a clean inch upon them from end to end.

"What a horrid mess!" cried the gardener's wife, who had been at first very angry, and then very frightened. "But I know what it is; that nasty Boxer has got loose again. It's he that has done it."

"Boxer wouldn't tie shirt-sleeves in double knots, or make balls of pocket-handkerchiefs," the gardener was heard to answer solemnly.

"Then it's those horrid children; they are always up to some mischief or other—just let me catch them!"

"You'd better not," said somebody in a voice exactly like the gardener's, though he himself declared he had not spoken a word. Indeed, he was fast asleep.

"Well, it's the most extraordinary thing I ever heard of," the gardener's wife said, supposing she was talking to her husband all the time; but soon she held her tongue, for she found here and there among the clothes all sorts of queer marks—marks of fingers, and toes, and heels, not in mud at all, but in coal-dust, as black as black could be.

Now, as the place where the big coal had tumbled out of the barrow was fully fifty yards from the orchard, and as the coal could not come to the clothes, and the clothes could not go without hands, the only conclusion she could arrive at was—well, no particular conclusion at all!

It was too late that night to begin washing again; besides, she was extremely tired, and her husband woke up rather worse than usual, so she just bundled the clothes up anyhow in a corner, put the kitchen to rights, and went mournfully to bed.

Next morning she got up long before it was light, washed her clothes through all over again, and it being impossible to dry them by the fire, went out with them once more, and began spreading them out in their usual corner, in a hopeless and melancholy manner. While she was at it, the little folks came trooping around her. She didn't scold them this time, she was too low-spirited.

"No! My old man isn't any better and I don't fancy he ever will be," said she, in answer to their questions. "And everything's going wrong with us—just listen!" And she told the trick which had been played her about the clothes.

The little people tried not to laugh, but it was so funny; and even now, the minute she had done hanging them out, there was something so droll in the way the clothes blew about, without any wind; the shirts hanging with their necks downward, as if there was a man inside them; and the drawers standing stiffly astride on the gooseberry-bushes, for all the world as if they held a pair of legs still. As for the gardener's nightcaps—long, white cotton, with a tassel at the top—they were alarming to look at; just like a head stuck on the top of a pole.

The whole thing was so peculiar, and the old woman so comical in her despair, that the children, after trying hard to keep it in, at last broke into shouts of laughter. She turned furiously upon them.

"It was you who did it!"

"No, indeed it wasn't," said they, jumping further to escape her blows. For she had got one of her clothes-props and was laying about her in the most reckless manner. However, she hurt nobody, and then she suddenly burst out, not laughing, but crying.

"It's a cruel thing, whoever has done it, to play such tricks on a poor old lady like me, with a sick husband that she works hard for, and not a child to help her. But I don't care. I'll wash my clothes again, if it's twenty times over, and I'll hang them out again in the very place, just to make you all ashamed of yourselves."

Perhaps the little people were ashamed of themselves, though they really had not done the mischief. But they knew quite well who had done it, and more than once they were about to tell; only they were afraid if they did so they should vex the Brownie so much that he would never come and play with them any more.

So they looked at one another without speaking, and when the gardener's wife had emptied her basket and dried her eyes, they said to her, very kindly:

"Perhaps no harm will come to your clothes this time. We'll sit and watch them till they are dry."

"Just as you like; I don't care. Them that hides can find, and them that plays tricks knows how to stop 'em."

It was not a civil speech, but then things were hard for the poor old woman. She had been awake nearly all night, and up washing at daybreak; her eyes were red with crying, and her steps weary and slow. The little children felt quite sorry for her, and instead of going to play sat watching the clothes as patiently as possible.

Nothing came near them. Sometimes, as before, the things seemed to dance about without hands and turn into odd shapes, as if there were people inside them; but not a creature was seen, and not a sound was heard. And though there was neither wind nor sun, very soon all the linen was perfectly dry.

"Fetch one of mother's baskets, and we'll fold it up as tidily as possible—that is, the girls can do it, it's their business—and we boys will carry it safe to the gardener's cottage."

So said they, not liking to say that they could not trust it out of their sight for fear of Brownie, whom, indeed, they were expecting to see peer round from every bush. They began to have a secret fear that he was rather a naughty Brownie, but then as the eldest little girl whispered, "He was only a Brownie, and knew no better." Now they were growing quite big children, who would be men and women some time; when they hoped they would never do anything wrong. (Their parents hoped the same, but doubted it.)

In a serious and careful manner they folded up the clothes and laid them one by one in the basket without any mischief, until, just as the two biggest boys were lifting their burden to carry it away, they felt something tugging at it from underneath.

"Halloo! Where are you taking all this rubbish? Better give it to me."

"No, if you please," said they very civilly, not to offend the little brown man. "We'll not trouble you, thanks! We'd rather do it ourselves; for the poor old gardener is very ill, and his wife is very miserable, and we are extremely sorry for them both."

"Extremely sorry!" cried Brownie, throwing up his cap in the air, and tumbling head over heels in an excited manner. "What in the world does extremely sorry mean?"

The children could not explain, especially to a Brownie; but they thought they understood—anyhow, they felt it. And they looked so sorrowful that the Brownie could not tell what to make of it.

He could not be said to be sorry, since, being a Brownie, and not a human being, knowing right from wrong, he never tried particularly to do right, and had no idea when he was doing wrong. But he seemed to have an idea that he was troubling the children, and he never liked to see them look unhappy.

So he turned head over heels six times running, and then came back again.

"The silly old woman! I washed her clothes for her last night in a way she didn't expect. I hadn't any soap, so I used a little mud and coal-dust, and very pretty they looked. Ha! ha! ha! Shall I wash them over again to-night?"

"Oh, no, please don't!" implored the children.

"Shall I starch and iron them? I'll do it beautifully. One—two—three, five—six—seven, Abracadabra, tum—tum—ti!" shouted he, jabbering all sorts of nonsense as it seemed to the children, and playing such antics that they stood and stared in the utmost amazement, and quite forgot the clothes. When they looked round again, the basket was gone.

"Seek till you find, seek till you find,
 Under the biggest gooseberry-bush, exactly to your mind."

They heard him singing this remarkable rhyme long after they had lost sight of him. And then they all set about searching; but it was a long while before they found, and still longer before they could decide, which was the biggest gooseberry-bush, each child having his or her opinion—sometimes a very strong one—on the matter. At last they agreed to settle it by pulling half a dozen little sticks, to see which stick was the longest, and the child that held it was to decide the gooseberry-bush.

This done, underneath the branches what should they find but the identical basket of clothes! Only, instead of being roughly dried, they were all starched and ironed in the most beautiful manner. As for the shirts, they really were a picture to behold, and the stockings were all folded up, and even darned in one or two places as neatly as possible. And strange to tell, there was not a single black mark of feet or fingers on any of them.

"Kind little Brownie! Clever little Brownie!" cried the children in chorus, and thought this was the most astonishing trick he had ever played.

What the gardener's wife said about it, whether they told her anything, or allowed her to suppose that the clothes had been done in their own laundry instead of the Brownie's (wherever that establishment might be), is more than I can tell. Of one thing only I am certain—that the little people said nothing but what was true. Also, that the very minute they got home they told their mother everything.

But for a long time after that they were a good deal troubled. The gardener got better, and went hobbling about the place again, to his own and everybody's great content, and his wife was less sharp-tongued and complaining than usual—indeed, she had nothing to complain of. All the family were very flourishing, except the little Brownie.

Often there was heard a curious sound all over the house; it might have been rats squeaking behind the wainscot—the elders said it was—but the children were sure it was a sort of weeping and wailing.

> "They've stolen my coal,
> And I haven't a hole
> To hide in;
> Not even a house
> One could ask a mouse
> To bide in."

A most forlorn tune it was, ending in a dreary minor key, and it lasted for months and months—at least the children said it did. And they were growing quite dull for want of a play-fellow, when, by the greatest good luck in the world, there came to the house not only a new lot of kittens, but a new baby. And the new baby was everybody's pet, including the Brownie's.

From that time, though he was not often seen, he was continually heard up and down the staircase, where he was frequently mistaken for Tiny or the cat, and sent sharply down again, which was wasting a great deal of wholesome anger upon Mr. Nobody. Or he lurked in odd corners of the nursery, whither the baby was seen crawling eagerly after nothing in particular, or sitting laughing with all her might at something —probably at her own toes.

But, as Brownie was never seen, he was never suspected. And since he did no mischief—neither pinched the baby nor broke the toys, left no soap in the bath and no foot-marks about the room—but was always a well-conducted Brownie in every way, he was allowed to inhabit the nursery (or supposed to do so, since, as nobody saw him, nobody could prevent him), until the children were grown up into men and women.

After that he retired into his coal-cellar, and for all I know he may live there still, and have gone through hundreds of adventures since; but as I never heard them, I can't tell them. Only I think if I could be a little child again, I should exceedingly like a Brownie to play with me. Should not you?